Sex Please We're Sixty

AN AMERICAN FARCE

by Michael Parker
and Susan Parker

A SAMUEL FRENCH ACTING EDITION

SAMUEL FRENCH

FOUNDED 1830

NEW YORK HOLLYWOOD LONDON TORONTO

SAMUELFRENCH.COM

ISBN 978-0-573-66386-4   Printed in U.S.A.   #20725

IMPORTANT BILLING AND CREDIT REQUIREMENTS

SEX PLEASE WE'RE SIXTY was first produced by Play With Your Food Productions in Hemet, California on October 17, 2008.

Cast:

BUD DAVIS . . . . Murray Robitaille

MRS. STANCLIFFE . . . . Corinne Williams

HENRY MITCHELL . . . . Richard Gordon

VICTORIA AMBROSE . . . . Janet Fulton

HILLARY HUDSON . . . . Marion Hair

CHARMAINE BEAUREGARD . . . . Judi Phares

Directed by Laura A. Robitaille
Designed by Kristina Lindholm, Murray Robiaille and Laura Robitaille

TIME

The Present

PLACE

Rose Cottage Bed & Breakfast...somewhere in New England

ACT I: Mid-summer afternoon
ACT II: Same time the next day

CHARACTERS

BUD DAVIS (Age 70 plus): The next-door neighbor to Mrs. Stancliffe's Rose Cottage Bed & Breakfast. He is weak, frail looking (*the frailer the better*), and appears at first glance to have "One foot in the grave." However, over the years, he has become renowned among the female guests as "Bud the Stud." He claims responsibility for the success of the bed & breakfast, believing all the females return year after year to see him. He enchants all of them with his silver tongue and sexual prowess. (*Very elderly, somewhat infirm, chauvinistic, brazen, but likeable.*)

MRS. STANCLIFFE (Age 60 plus): The owner of Rose Cottage Bed & Breakfast. She is a severe woman both in dress and manner. Precise in speech and punctuality, she gives the impression of efficiency and competence. She is intolerant of Bud's "Hanky-Panky", with her guests, but reluctantly has to agree he is good for business. Pursued by her next-door neighbor Henry, she refuses to let him into her life, until surprising events finally bring them together. (*Sensible, practical, punctual, business like, menopausal, finally radiant and sensuous.*)

HENRY MITCHELL (Age 60 plus): A retired chemist and Mrs. Stancliffe's "Gentleman Caller." He is a mild mannered man who has proposed to Mrs. Stancliffe every afternoon for twenty years. He is always the perfect gentleman, and shows a great deal of respect for all the women around him. He has developed Venusia, a pill to increase the libido in menopausal women, but refuses to test it on moral grounds. Bud calls him, "A stick in the mud.", and he probably is, but eventually comes out of his shell. (*Gentle, caring, thoughtful, loveable.*)

VICTORIA AMBROSE (Age 50 plus): Victoria is a renowned author who writes steamy romantic novels. She pines for romance in her personal life, but finds none. Flattered at first by Bud's attentions, she later sees him as the shallow, insincere Casanova that he really is and readily joins the plot to turn "Bud the Stud" into "Bud the Dud." (*Pretty, serious, intelligent, menopausal.*)

HILLARY HUDSON (Age 50 plus): Hillary is beautiful, well educated, articulate and sophisticated in both manner and dress. She is an old friend and co-worker of Henry's, who agrees to test the Venusia pills. Initially skeptical of Bud's attentions, she gradually warms towards him, but is it the Venusia or Bud's charms? *(Elegant, charming, best described as "A touch of class", intelligent and menopausal.)*

CHARMAINE BEAUREGARD (Age 50 plus): Charmaine is the quintessential southern belle. She is definitely here at Rose Cottage for "Bud the Stud." Of all people, she does not need Venusia, as her entire life seems to be run by her overactive libido. However, she is a proud woman who will not be two-timed by Bud, and becomes the leading light in the plot to tame him. *(Voluptuous, out-going, gushing, demonstrative, menopausal.)*

ACT 1

It is a mid-summer afternoon at Rose Cottage, somewhere in New England. The time is 4:37 PM. The curtain rises on an empty set. It is the living room and breakfast nook of Mrs. Stancliffe's Rose Cottage Bed & Breakfast. D.R. is a set of French doors leading to the garden. The doors are slightly open. Above them is the door to bedroom one, and above that, a small built in counter, which serves as the reception desk for the bed and breakfast. On the counter is the reservations computer notebook, a call bell, a telephone and an empty vase with water. Behind the counter is an open archway leading to Mrs. Stancliffe's office. U.C. is an opening containing a large potted plant, which leads off right to the front door. The whole U.L. area is the breakfast nook. It is on a platform raised one or two steps, with railings R. and D.L. The nook has a round table, 3 chairs and a small buffet, with a jug of iced tea and glasses on it. On the U.S. wall of the nook is another set of French doors, which open onto a flower garden. U.L. is an open archway leading to the kitchen. Below the nook on the left wall, is the door to bedroom two, and below that, the door to bedroom three. C.S. is a sofa and a low back easy chair, with a small table between them.

The décor is bright and cheerful. Sunlight streams in through the French doors.

*There are country cottage paintings, flowered drapes and valances. There is a vase of fresh flowers on the center stage table. After a moment or two, **BUD DAVIS** appears in the D.R. French doors. **BUD** is a slight, frail looking man, age perhaps 70 – 80. Despite his appearance, his successful amorous pursuits of Mrs. Stancliffe's female guests have created an image of himself as "Bud the*

Stud." Bud only ever has one thing on his mind...his next conquest. He is wearing a short sleeve plaid shirt and khaki pants, which are pulled up high on his waist, a sweater vest, and a golf cap. He looks around, and, seeing no one, moves towards the reservation desk and begins to search through the computer.

Enter **MRS. STANCLIFFE** *from the nook French doors, with a basket of fresh cut flowers from the garden and a pair of scissors.* **MRS. STANCLIFFE** *is in her sixties. She is a plain looking woman, with her hair, worn either in a French bun, or similar severe manner. She wears no make-up or jewelry, except for a watch. She is wearing a long, dull colored plain dress, ankle boots, and garden gloves.* **MRS. STANCLIFFE** *has a penchant for punctuality, uses precise, articulate speech, and has a no-nonsense approach to life in general.*

MRS. STANCLIFFE. *(Quickly crosses R.)* Mr. Bud Davis, just exactly what do you think you are doing?

BUD. What does it look like I'm doing? It's what I do every afternoon checking the reservations to see if any of my "chicks" are arriving today.

MRS. STANCLIFFE. *(Now at the counter, closes the computer, almost on Bud's fingers.)* Mr. Davis, I run a respectable bed & breakfast. There are no "chicks", as you so crudely call them.

BUD. Oh, come on Mrs. Stancliffe, you know the only reason your bed & breakfast is so popular is because of "Bud the Stud." Why else do you think they come back year after year?

MRS. STANCLIFFE. I know of no such thing, and I wish you to refrain from using that vile phrase. The only thing we ever have in common is our mutual hobby, gardening. I have accepted your presence at my establishment for these past 20 years because you are my next-door neighbor, and were a friend of my late husband. For heaven's sake Bud, why can't you just be friends with my guests?

BUD. What?

MRS. STANCLIFFE. What do you call people you meet socially, and don't try to get into bed?

BUD. Men?

MRS. STANCLIFFE. You are impossible. You know I do not approve of any form of hanky-panky with my guests.

BUD. *(To himself)* Maybe if you'd participate you'd be a little less uptight?

MRS. STANCLIFFE. What's that?

BUD. I said, "I'd like to date a guest tonight."

MRS. STANCLIFFE. You are incorrigible. However, I must reluctantly admit, that many of my guests, for some extraordinary reason, do seem to find you irresistible.

BUD. So, you admit I'm good for business. Can I get at the booking page now?

MRS. STANCLIFFE: Certainly not! I do, however, have a message for you. At precisely 7:47 post meridian, yesterday, one of your former paramours left you a message. She will be arriving today, and wishes to re-acquaint herself with you.

BUD: See, I told you, they all come back to "Bud the Stud". Now, what's her name?

MRS. STANCLIFFE. I am not your booking agent. Suffice it to say, I have delivered the message.

BUD. How am suppose to re-acquaint myself with her if I don't know who she is.

MRS. STANCLIFFE. I refuse to make your appointments for you, but I will tell you that the lady in question referred to you as *(Rolls her eyes)* "Studly Budly Do-right."

BUD. Well, that doesn't help me at all, they all call me that.

MRS. STANCLIFFE. How you can have a romantic liaison with someone, and not remember her name, is completely beyond my comprehension.

BUD. What's sex got to do with remembering their names? I can't even remember what I had for breakfast.

MRS. STANCLIFFE. Really Mr. Davis. Do you ever have a thought that originates above the waist? Have you nothing better to do with your time than stand here waiting to look at my reservations?

BUD. Have I ever told you-

MRS. STANCLIFFE. No, and don't start now.

BUD. *(Smiling.)* Right Mrs. S. Well, if there's at least one chick coming in today, I'd better go replenish my stock of condoms. *(He pronounces this word with the emphasis on the second syllable.)*

MRS. STANCLIFFE. That is quite enough, and for heaven's sake stop smiling. You look like the Mona Lisa on valium. Mr. Davis, I am terminating this conversation at precisely *(Looks at her watch)* 4:41 post meridian.

BUD. Well, with at least one chick coming in, it looks like it is going to be a good day. *(Heads towards the DR French doors.)*

MRS. STANCLIFFE. Before you leave, I would like to talk with you about your hobby.

BUD. *(Now almost out of the doors, and not heard by* **MRS. STAN-CLIFFE.***)* My hobby is sex. *(Turns.)* You want to talk about my hobby?

MRS. STANCLIFFE. Yes, I do.

BUD. You're not embarrassed to talk about this with me?

MRS. STANCLIFFE. *(Comes D. to the couch L. side.)* Not at all. I accept the fact that you have been doing it longer than me, and are more knowledgeable and experienced than I am. Please, sit for a moment. (**BUD** *sits in the chair.)* Much as I love it, I know I'm not very good at it.

BUD. You do? You're not?

MRS. STANCLIFFE. Well, I have a little success every now and again, but I have noticed that you seem to have a certain touch.

BUD. It all comes with experience Mrs. S.

MRS. STANCLIFFE. That's it exactly. I realize I need to learn from you in order to improve my skills.

BUD. You want to improve your skills?

MRS. STANCLIFFE. Why not, you're never too old to learn, and I'm sure you're a great teacher.

BUD. You want me to teach you?

MRS. STANCLIFFE. Yes, I have exactly 4 and ¾ minutes, if you have the time, we could do it now.

BUD. Do it? Now? In 4 and ¾ minutes?

MRS. STANCLIFFE. Yes, why don't we go out to the garden and you can show me a thing or two?

BUD. *(Stands.)* Show you a thing or two? In the garden? I don't think so Mrs. S. I am terminating this conversation, now. *(Runs out the DR French doors.)*

MRS. STANCLIFFE. *(Moves U.S. to the counter.)* What in heaven's name got into him?

*(Enter **HENRY** from the U.L. French doors. Henry, now in his sixties, is a retired chemist. He is an attractive man, with a gentle personality. He wears a polo shirt with khaki pants. Henry has persistently and patiently, courted and proposed to Mrs. Stancliffe, every day for the past twenty years. He arrives daily with a different flower for each day of the week. To-day they are carnations.)*

HENRY. *(Crossing R. to the counter.)* My dear Mrs. Stancliffe, you look as radiant as a rosebud this afternoon. Will you do me the honor of becoming my wife?

MRS. STANCLIFFE. Henry, you've asked me that same question every day for the past twenty years. *(Looks at her watch.)* Though you are precisely one and three-quarter minutes later than usual today.

HENRY. I do so humbly apologize. I seem to be moving a little slowly today.

MRS. STANCLIFFE. Henry, my answer will be the same as it was yesterday. I am over forty you know, and at our time of life we should not rush into things. While I continue to grow extremely fond of you, I need time to consider your proposal.

HENRY. *(Hands her the flowers.)* Very well my dear.

MRS. STANCLIFFE. Ah, carnations, it must be Friday. *(Puts the flowers into the empty vase)*

HENRY. I understand my dear that if you need time, you need time but, in the mean time, you're not getting any younger.

MRS. STANCLIFFE. Really? And who do you think you are, Peter Pan?

HENRY. You are, of course, right my dear, but I must admit, besides our long term friendship, I do have a strong physical attraction for you.

MRS. STANCLIFFE. Me?

HENRY. Yes, you my dear. *(Pats her hand.)* I hope I didn't shock you, but I remember a conversation we had quite a while ago, when you told me that after your husband died, you too, on occasion, had felt the need for more than...how shall I put this...just friendship. He's been dead for over twenty-five years now, don't you think....

MRS. STANCLIFFE. *(Quickly withdraws her hand.)* No, and I don't think you should either. I have absolutely no recollection of any such conversation. However, while we're on the subject, Bud is getting out of hand. He seems to think he's a one man geriatric sexual revolution. He is soliciting my guests on a daily basis. You are a retired chemist. Isn't there some pill you can give him to control his over active libido?

HENRY. *(Laughing.)* I'm afraid not my dear, except perhaps taking a cold shower, and heaven knows, I've had plenty of those. As a matter of fact, I have been doing research in the exact opposite direction. I have been working on a pill that will increase the libido in....

MRS. STANCLIFFE. I find this an entirely inappropriate conversation, and am terminating it at precisely *(Looks at her watch.)* 4:44 post-meridian. There is your usual iced-tea on the buffet. If you'll excuse me for a moment, I need to attend to these flowers, and take care of one other small matter. I shall return in precisely three and one half minutes for our usual afternoon iced-tea together. *(Exits to office, with the basket of flowers and the scissors.)*

*(**HENRY** crosses L. to nook, pours himself an iced-tea, and sits in the U.S. chair, as **BUD** enters from the D.R. French doors and heads to the counter.)*

BUD. Hi Henry, how you doing?

HENRY. Good afternoon Bud. I'm fine, thank you. What are you doing?

BUD. *(At the computer.)* Checking the reservation page to see which one of my chicks is checking in today.

HENRY. You'd better watch out, Mrs. Stancliffe's on the warpath, she seems hormonally challenged today. You'd better not get caught.

BUD. You mean she didn't take her cranky pill? Still, with her how can you tell? Anyway, I'm not worried, she knows I do this. She doesn't even have a password to keep me out. She knows that "Bud the Stud" is what keeps this place going. *(Checking computer.)* Any luck with your proposal today? Has the iceberg thawed out?

HENRY. No, I'm afraid nothing has changed. It's the same old story. For twenty years, I propose, she says she needs more time and in the meantime, we're running out of time. By the time she says yes, we'll be so old, we'll need separate honeymoons. To be honest, I've been thinking about taking a desperate measure.

BUD. *(Frowning at the computer.)* There are three check-ins today, and I know at least one of them is a chick of mine, but I don't remember any of the names. Oh well, as long as everything is working, except my memory, I'm still hot to trot. *(Crossing L. to the buffet, pours himself an iced-tea and sits L. chair.)* So, what's this about desperate measures?

HENRY. Well last year, as you know, I went on vacation to the South of Italy.

BUD. Yes.

HENRY. Well, I saw some peppers advertised as a natural Viagra for menopausal women who have lost their sex drive. It occurred to me, that this was a huge opportunity to create a pill to help boost a woman's libido. So, I bought a whole bunch of them, brought them back with me, and extracted the enzymes in my lab. I've now got them into a concentrated formula contained in this small blue pill, and I have been wondering if I should ask Mrs. Stancliffe to take one. *(Takes a bottle out of his pocket, shows them to Bud, and puts them on the table.)*

BUD. Oh, they look just like my…. *(Pauses.)*

HENRY. Your what?

BUD. Never mind.

HENRY. I've patented the formula, and registered the name. It's called Venusia.

BUD. Venusia?

HENRY. Yes, Venusia, named after Venus the goddess of love.

BUD. Well, does it work?

HENRY. I don't know, I haven't had a chance to test them out yet. How would you like to test them out on some of your female friends.

BUD. They don't need anything like that, they've got "Bud the Stud." Why don't you try it out on the iceberg? Just slip it in a drink and don't tell her? What have you got to lose?

HENRY. Oh no, I couldn't do that. She'd have to know about it. Without her consent it would be unethical and immoral.

BUD. We're talking about sex. What do ethics and morality have to do with it?

HENRY. Well to be honest, the thought did cross my mind, but it would be wrong.

BUD. Then do it in the name of science. It won't be a fair test if the person trying it knows. It might alter the results.

HENRY. You've got a point Bud, I'll give it some thought.

BUD. Oh, Henry, you're such a stick in the mud.

HENRY. What do you mean?

BUD. You follow the exact same routine every single day of your life, you won't try the Venusia on Mrs. S., you don't seem to understand that the secret to getting chicks is to sweep them off their feet. Take the plunge, for heaven's sake, do something different.

HENRY. I don't want chicks, just Mrs. Stancliffe.

BUD. Then do something different.

HENRY. Well, I guess it couldn't hurt. As a matter of fact, I have been mulling over doing something quite daring and different. I'll be back in a jiffy. *(Exits U.S. French doors, leaving the pill bottle on the table.)*

*(**BUD** watches him leave, opens the pill bottle, slips a few into his pocket, then hastily puts the cap back on the bottle as **HENRY** re-enters from the French doors.)*

HENRY. *(Seeing the pill bottle in **BUD**'s hand.)* I think I'd better have those Bud. *(Takes the pill bottle and exits French doors.)*

BUD. *(Watches Henry leave, takes one of the Venusia pills out of his pocket, moves to the buffet, pours a glass of tea, drops the Venusia pill in it, stirs frantically, and turns R. with the glass in his hand.)* Oh, Mrs. Stancliffe.

*(Enter **VICTORIA** through the front door. A mature woman 50 plus, wearing a modest summer dress, carrying a computer bag and small suitcase. Her prim and proper appearance and manner belie the fact that she is, in fact, a romance novelist. **BUD** sees her, puts the glass down on the buffet, and rushes over to greet her.)*

BUD. Here, let me help you with that. *(Takes her luggage from her.)* You look familiar, have we met before?

VICTORIA. You don't remember me?

BUD. Er… er…of course I do. How could I forget you?

VICTORIA. Well, the time we spent together last year was fairly brief.

BUD. I know, but how could I ever forget such a vision of loveliness, such beauty, such charm. I have dreamed about you many times in the past year, but the face in my dreams was never as beautiful as the one I see before me today.

VICTORIA. Oh really?

BUD. I would very much like to renew our acquaintance this evening. *(He starts to bow)* Perhaps over a glass of champagne, with a little caviar, in the moonlight?

(BUD raises his right hand above his head, takes one step back with his right foot, makes a sweeping gesture with the right hand while bending his right knee. His right hand sweeps down to his right foot in a bowing gesture. Immediately he grabs his back with his left hand and stays in this bent position. There is a long pause.)

VICTORIA. That is an impressive bow Mr. Davis.

BUD. *(Still in the position.)* Thank you.

VICTORIA. It's alright if you'd like to stand up now.

BUD. Well, that's a problem. I seem to be having some difficulty with my back.

VICTORIA. *(She bends down to talk to him, so her head is about an inch from his.)* May I help you?

BUD. You could try to straighten me up.

(VICTORIA comes behind him and puts her head and shoulders underneath his right armpit and attempts to raise him up. They struggle and she slowly succeeds. However, as his right side rises, his left side gets lower and lower. The net result is that he ends up in the exact same position, only the left side is down and the right side is up. She stands back and looks at him.)

VICTORIA. I have an idea, let's get you over to the couch.

(VICTORIA comes behind him again, this time going under his left arm and together they shuffle down to the front of the couch. BUD manages to get his left hand on the cushion of the couch, supporting some of his weight. VICTORIA goes behind him and tries to pull his shoulder

up, but it doesn't work. She then slides beneath him on her back on the couch, then, with her feet on his chest, attempts to push him straight up. His back straightens up, but **BUD** *collapses on top of her as* **MRS. STANCLIFFE** *enters from the office. She comes D. behind the couch, and with arms folded, gives them a disapproving glare.)*

BUD. Hi there Mrs. S. *(***MRS. STANCLIFFE** *continues to glare.)* Lovely afternoon, isn't it? *(***MRS. STANCLIFFE** *rolls her eyes.)*

VICTORIA. *(Pushes* **BUD** *off her, and he falls on the floor as she gets up.)* I'm so sorry Mrs. Stancliffe. *(***MRS. STAN-CLIFFE** *nods.)* I was simply trying to help him with his back. I don't know if you remember me, I'm Victoria Ambrose. I have a reservation.

MRS. STANCLIFFE. Welcome back to Rose Cottage.

BUD. Roses, that's it roses, champagne, caviar. *(Kisses Victoria's hand from the floor and stands up.)* Au Revoir ma cherie. *(Exits jauntily out the French doors R.)*

MRS. STANCLIFFE. I apologize for Mr. Davis. I do hope he wasn't bothering you.

VICTORIA. Not exactly, I met him briefly when I was here last year. I remember him being quite a character. Apparently he hasn't changed, instead of growing old gracefully, he's decided to grow old disgracefully.

MRS. STANCLIFFE. He is definitely a unique individual, I will say that. Now, Ms. Ambrose, shall we get you checked in? *(***VICTORIA** *nods as* **MRS. STANCLIFFE** *hands her a card.)* Victoria Ambrose…I hope I am not being too forward, I know you've been a guest here before, but your name does seem very familiar.

VICTORIA. Perhaps you recognize my name from one of my novels.

MRS. STANCLIFFE. That's it. *(Looks around.)* I must admit, I do, on occasion, indulge in a romance novel or two. I have read several of yours…very racy I might add. Are you working on anything new?

VICTORIA. As a matter of fact that's why I'm here. I have a deadline to meet from my publisher, and I'm struggling a little to get my newest one completed. I'm hoping that a few days of peace and quiet here will allow me to finish it.

MRS. STANCLIFFE. It must be hard to find the right words all the time.

VICTORIA. Well, sometimes yes, but in this case, it's not so much the words, as much as I need to find a way to bring the lovers together after three hundred pages of misunderstandings have kept them apart. What I really need to come up with is a new and original idea that rings true to life.

MRS. STANCLIFFE. I'm sure you'll find it in the peace and quiet of Rose Cottage.

VICTORIA. Let's hope so.

MRS. STANCLIFFE If it's not too bold, may I take a peek at this latest one sometime?

VICTORIA. Not at all. *(Opening up her computer bag)* Most of it is still on the computer, but I have printed out the first few pages that I can let you look at. *(Hands papers to Mrs. Stancliffe, who sets them on the counter.)*

MRS.STANCLIFFE. Thank you, I will look forward to reading them. So, shall we finish getting you checked in. I just need you to sign this form. *(***VICTORIA** *signs it and hands it to* **MRS. STANCLIFFE.***)* You will be in the Cajun Sunrise Rose room. *(Puts the card under the desk, and hands her a key.)* I was just about to have a glass of iced-tea with my gentleman caller, *(Looks at her watch.)* who appears to be late. Would you care to join me before you go to your room?

(Picks up the novel pages and crosses L. to the nook.)

VICTORIA. Thank you that would be nice. *(Follows her left and sits in the R. chair.)* So, a gentleman caller? Sounds exciting.

MRS. STANCLIFFE. *(She sets the papers on the table, turns to the buffet, sees the glass that* **BUD** *poured, and with her back* *to the audience, pours another glass.)* Henry, exciting? Those are not the words I would use to describe him. Although I am extremely fond of him, we seem to be lacking the passion that your characters exhibit in their relationships. I must admit, that for the past few years, since the onset of "the change", I've not really felt much passion at all. I guess it is to be expected at my time of life. *(She then turns R. to* **VICTORIA***, with a glass in each hand. The audience must not see which glass is which.)* Here you are. *(Hands her a glass, sits in the L. chair and sips her tea as she picks up the pages and begins reading.)*

VICTORIA. I know exactly what you mean.

MRS. STANCLIFFE. *(Begins to fan herself.)* Oh dear, here I go again. One minute I'm just fine and the next, I feel like a roasting marshmallow.

VICTORIA. *(Laughing.)* Been there, done that. I was hoping it was what you were reading that made you hot under the collar. For me, it's the night-time hot flashes that are the worst. What I wouldn't give for one good night's sleep without waking up drenched. You know, I've often wondered, if men had hot flashes instead of women, what it would do to their libido? I mean, it just doesn't seem fair.

MRS. STANCLIFFE. I know….*(Who has been looking at the manuscript on and off.)* Oh my goodness, how do you manage to write such words?

VICTORIA. *(Sipping the tea.)* What are you talking about?

MRS. STANCLIFFE. *(Reading aloud.)* "He placed his hand upon her silken thigh and sent tremors through her heaving bosom."

VICTORIA. It does sound a bit much, doesn't it?

MRS. STANCLIFFE. *(Laughing.)* Oh no, I love it! *(Reading aloud.)* "Her dark brown eyes glistened in the moon-light and her ruby red lips trembled as his manhood pressed against her."

VICTORIA. I'm glad you're enjoying it.

MRS. STANCLIFFE. I see here you've used your own name, Victoria, for one of your characters.

VICTORIA. Yes. This is the first time I've ever done that in one of my novels. I must admit though, the character is nothing at all like me. *(Yawns.)* Please excuse me, I guess I'm feeling a little tired after my long drive here.

MRS. STANCLIFFE. Why don't you go lie down for a while. Here, let me help you. *(She picks up the suitcase, crosses R. to the door of bedroom 1 and opens the door.)* It's a lovely room, I'm sure you'll be quite comfortable in here.

VICTORIA. *(Carrying her glass of tea, she follows her R. and takes the suitcase.)* You can return the manuscript pages when you're finished reading them. *(Exits to bedroom 1, closing the door.)*

(MRS. STANCLIFFE hurries back to the table and eagerly grabs the papers, sits in the R. chair and begins to read the manuscript. Enter HILLARY through the front entrance way. Age fifty plus, she is an attractive woman with a classic style. She is wearing a designer summer suit, accessories and shoes to match. She is carrying a purse and a small suitcase. She pauses and watches as MRS. STANCLIFFE continues to read.)

MRS. STANCLIFFE. *(Reading.)* "Oh my goodness……. Oh my……. Oh no,…..He did what?,……He put his hand where?…..Oh my…. Well I never knew that was possible……Ooooh!

(Eventually HILLARY moves R. and rings the call bell. MRS. STANCLIFFE, startled, jumps up, leaving the manuscript on the table.)

MRS. STANCLIFFE. *(Crosses R.)* I am so sorry, I didn't hear you come in.

HILLARY. I'm not surprised, you were obviously reading something that had you totally engrossed.

MRS. STANCLIFFE. Ah, yes, well, welcome to Rose Cottage. *(Shakes hands with Hillary.)* I am Mrs. Stancliffe, the proprietress.

HILLARY. Hello, I'm Hillary Hudson. I have a reservation.

*(**MRS. STANCLIFFE** moves behind the counter, as **BUD** is about to enter the D.R. French doors. He has a bottle of champagne in one hand and roses in the other. He stops dead in his tracks. He should be visible to the audience, but not to **MRS. STANCLIFFE** and **HILLARY**. He listens intently.)*

MRS. STANCLIFFE. *(Hands **HILLARY** a reservation card.)* If you wouldn't mind just filling in this form. Is this the first time you've stayed at Rose Cottage?

HILLARY. Yes it is. A friend of mine told me about this place, and said it was wonderfully romantic. *(Bud reacts.)*

MRS. STANCLIFFE. I am pleased to hear that. I think!

HILLARY. You see, I've been widowed for a few years now, and haven't really had much of a social life. My friend suggested that it was time I started to get out and meet people again. So, here I am. *(Bud reacts.)*

MRS. STANCLIFFE. I hope that we can live up to your expectations. *(Bud reacts.)*

HILLARY. At my age, the only expectation I have is to not have expectations.

MRS. STANCLIFFE. I know exactly what you mean my dear. However, I do have an expectation of a gentleman caller every afternoon at precisely 4:42 post meridian.

HILLARY. Mmmm, a gentleman caller. Well, this place certainly sounds romantic. Maybe I will meet someone here.

BUD. *(Moves U.S. towards **HILLARY** with wine and roses.)* My dear Mrs. Stancliffe, I beg of you, introduce me to this vision of loveliness. *(Turns to **HILLARY**.)* Never in my dreams have I seen such beauty, such charm. But the face in my dreams was never as beautiful as the one I see before me now.

MRS. STANCLIFFE. *(Rolling her eyes.)* Mrs. Hudson, may I introduce you to Mr. Bud Davis.

HILLARY. Hello *(Holds out her hand to shake hands with **BUD**.)*

BUD. *(With some difficulty drops down to one knee and kisses her hand.)* Bonjour, Ma Cherie.

HILLARY. Oh my! *(To **MRS. STANCLIFFE**.)* Do you welcome all of your guests this way?

BUD. *(Getting to his feet with some difficulty.)* Only those whose radiance outshines the sun.

MRS. STANCLIFFE. Oh for heaven's sake Bud.

BUD. *(Hands **HILLARY** the roses and wine.)* Red roses and wine for you my dear. Please accept them and enjoy their beauty, as I am enjoying yours. And perhaps I might drop by later and share a glass with you?

HILLARY. Oh my!

MRS. STANCLIFFE. Oh Bud, do behave yourself. *(To **HILLARY**.)* I must apologize for my neighbor. He does get a little carried away.

BUD. *(To Hillary.)* I am only carried away by the starlight I see in your eyes.

HILLARY. Oh my!

MRS. STANCLIFFE. Bud, why don't you make yourself useful and carry Mrs. Hudson's luggage to her room. *(To **HILLARY**.)* You will be in the Cherokee Rose room. If you need anything, please let me know. And Bud, I expect you to be on your best behavior.

BUD. When have I ever not been on my best behavior? *(**MRS. STANCLIFFE** opens her mouth about to answer.)* Don't answer that.

*(**MRS. STANCLIFFE** exits with the reservation form into the office, as **BUD** attempts to pick up **HILLARY**'s suitcase. He manages to get it about one inch in the air, before it falls back down again. He tries again, unsuccessfully.)*

HILLARY. Really, that's not necessary.

BUD. It's not that it's heavy, I just need to conserve my energy for later. *(He now begins to push it L. to bedroom 2, with great difficulty.)*

HILLARY. That's really very kind, but I can do it.

BUD. No, no, I've got it. *(Now about half-way to the door.)* Just give me half a minute. *(He stops and sits on the suitcase, huffing and puffing.)*

HILLARY. You really are quite the gentleman, aren't you Mr. Davis?

BUD. *(Stands and begins to pull the luggage.)* Anything to stay close to someone more beautiful than Venus, the goddess of love.

HILLARY. Oh my!

BUD. *(Now with the luggage outside the door to bedroom 2.)* I will be counting the moments until I see you again. Au Revoir, ma petite chou. *(Pronounced "shoe")*

(He raises his right arm above his head and moves his right leg back, beginning the bow routine again, but this time his back goes out while he is in the upright position, with his arm locked over his head and his face turned upward. There is a long pause while he remains motionless in this position.)

HILLARY. *(Looks up trying to see what **BUD** is looking at. She looks at him quizzically, then moves very close to him, turning so that her back is next to his chest, and looks upwards.)* What are you looking at?

BUD. Looking at?…Oh..oh the figure I see before me, the smile, the grace, the unparalleled beauty of a woman……

HILLARY. *(Turns to face **BUD** and in doing so knocks him in the stomach with her elbow. He places his left hand on his stomach, his right arm still up in the air.)* Oh, I'm sorry, are you all right?

BUD. *(Turns his left palm up and out a little in front of his stomach.)* I'm….I'm fine, just practicing my Shakespeare. "Shall I compare thee to a summer's day? Thou art more lovely and more temperate."

HILLARY. Really Mr. Davis, I don't think I've ever met anyone quite like you.

BUD. OOOH, OOOH *(Screams out as he unsuccessfully attempts to move his arm down.)* I seem to be having a little difficulty with my back.

HILLARY. *(Moves towards him, puts the wine on the floor and the roses on the suitcase.)* Mr. Davis, you should have told me right away. My late husband had back problems, and I was always able to help him. Now, we just need to get you on the couch.

BUD. Sounds good to me, but wouldn't a bed work better?

HILLARY. Mr. Davis, we are talking about your back. Not some weird, erotic fantasy you may have about me.

BUD. OK, the couch it is.

*(**HILLARY** guides him as he shuffles backwards, still in a totally rigid position, to the front center of the couch. He is facing D.R. She then goes behind him and takes his shoulders. He manages to bend his left leg, and she lowers him onto the couch, with his right arm still in the air, and his right leg rigid. She then grabs his shoulders and rolls him D.S. To prevent him falling off the couch, she grabs the waistband of his pants. As she lowers him to the floor, the pants slide down revealing boxer shorts with bright red hearts all over them. His right arm remains above his head and his right leg remains rigid. As he reaches the floor, **HILLARY** stumbles and falls on top of him.)*

HILLARY. Ohhh….Ohhhh…. Ohhhh no. *(She manages to sit up on top of Bud, straddling his behind.)*

MRS. STANCLIFFE. *(Hearing **HILLARY**, she rushes in from the office, comes D. behind the couch and pauses for a moment. **BUD** and **HILLARY** look up and smile, **BUD** gives a little finger wave as **MRS. STANCLIFFE** rolls her eyes.)* Mr. Davis, this was not what I meant when I asked you to make yourself useful. I shall return in precisely 2 minutes, at which time I expect proper decorum to be re-established in my living room. *(She tosses her head and quickly returns to the office.)*

HILLARY. OK Mr. Davis, let's get this done. Please take a deep breath and try to relax. *(She pushes down firmly with both hands on his upper back. **BUD** yells and **HILLARY** stands up.)*

BUD. *(Quickly stands up, rubbing his back.)* My goodness, that was amazing, how did you do that?

HILLARY. Oh it's nothing, I've had lots of practice.

BUD. Well, thank you. Maybe you'd like to meet up later for some more practice?

HILLARY. I don't think so Mr. Davis. Good evening. *(Easily picks up the luggage, takes the wine and roses with her, and exits bedroom 2, closing the door.)*

BUD. *(Moves U.S. towards the buffet, when he notices the manuscript pages on the table. He picks them up and starts to read.)* "THE SUMMER COTTAGE, MY JOURNEY OF LOVE", by Victoria Ambrose. *(Reads silently for a moment.)* "What we shared a year ago, compelled me to return to this simple cottage of love, and the man of my dreams." *(***BUD**, *looks at door to bedroom 1.)* It has to be her. I knew it, they all come back to Bud the Stud. *(Continues reading.)* "In the throes of passion he cried out my name, Oh Victoria, Victoria". Well, at least I got the name right. *(Continues to read.)* "I have counted the weeks, the days, the minutes until I would be back in the strong arms of the man I adore." *(***BUD** *flexes his arms and does a muscle pose.)* I always knew I was good, but they're even writing about me now! *(Continues reading.)*

(Enter **HENRY** *through the nook French doors, carrying a bouquet of pansies.)*

HENRY. So Bud, what do you think?

BUD. *(Continues to read without looking up.)* About what?

HENRY. *(Holds out bouquet to Bud.)* About these?

BUD. *(Looks up.)* Thanks, but no thanks. *(Continues reading.)*

HENRY. No, not for you, for Mrs. Stancliffe. They're tomorrow's flowers today. That should take her by surprise, sweep her off her feet.

BUD. *(Looks up.)* You've really gone all out Henry. You know what your problem is?

HENRY. I only have one?

BUD. Henry, you're about as romantic as a frozen fish. *(Waves the paper in* **HENRY**'s *face, then throws it on the table, and stands.)* Take lessons from a master my boy. While you play with your pansies, I've got a really hot chick who's been writing about me. *(Moves D.R.)* And now it looks like I might have two chicks, so I'd better go check on the condom reserves, and I'll definitely need some roses and champagne for Victoria. See Henry, if you're going to do it, do it with panache. *(Exits French doors R.)*

HENRY. Pansies are panache. *(Sits L. chair, and starts to read the paper on the table.)*

(Enter **VICTORIA** *from bedroom1, a pencil stuck in her hair and carrying an empty glass.)*

VICTORIA. *(Sees* **HENRY**.*)* Hello.

HENRY. *(Stands.)* Hello, I'm Henry Mitchell. May I pour you a glass of iced-tea?

VICTORIA. *(Crosses R. to the nook and hands glass to* **HENRY** *then sits on the R. chair.)* Yes, thank you. I'm Victoria Ambrose. Oh goodness, Mrs. Stancliffe left my manuscript on the table. You must be her gentleman caller.

HENRY. You're a writer?

VICTORIA. Yes, romance novels. I don't think the term gentleman caller has been used since the 1800's.

HENRY. *(Laughing, pours a glass of tea and hands it to* **VICTORIA**.*)* You're probably right. I'd like to be called her husband, but I'm afraid that gentleman caller is all I'm ever going to be.

VICTORIA. What makes you say that?

HENRY. I've been courting her for twenty years. I propose to her every day, and I get precisely nowhere. Did you say Mrs. Stancliffe was reading this?

VICTORIA. Yes, why?

HENRY. Well, she doesn't seem very interested in romance, at least not with me. Maybe I don't use the right words.

VICTORIA. Well, she was certainly enjoying what she was reading. Maybe I can help you with the words. I am a writer after all. Now tell me, what do you say when you propose?

HENRY. The same thing I say every day. "Mrs. Stancliffe, would you do me the honor of becoming my wife?"

VICTORIA. Oh dear.

HENRY. Oh dear?

VICTORIA. Oh dear. First of all, does she have a first name?

HENRY. Of course, it's Buttercup.

VICTORIA. Buttercup?

HENRY. Buttercup.

VICTORIA. O.K., let's go with that. Now, do you think you could manage something like this? Oh my beautiful Buttercup, when you look at me my heart skips a beat, and my passion knows no bounds. Whenever I see you I stop breathing.

HENRY. Hold on a second, let me write this down. *(Takes the pencil from Victoria's hair, and starts frantically writing on the back of one of the sheets.)*

VICTORIA. I cannot stand the thought of us being apart one more moment. I must taste those ruby lips, feel the softness of your tender touch, I cannot live another moment without knowing you will be mine forever. Please, make me the happiest of men and say you will be my wife.

HENRY. *(Pauses.)* Women like that kind of stuff?

VICTORIA. Well, I think so, I've sold over a million books. So, what have you got to lose? The next time you propose, give it a try. Oh, and getting down on one knee wouldn't hurt either.

HENRY. You must lead such an exciting and romantic life.

VICTORIA. Not at all. The novels are full of passion and romance, but my personal life is most definitely not.

HENRY. But Bud said that you,…that he, …that you and Bud were….um you know…um

VICTORIA. Ahh! Absolutely not. As a matter of fact, I found him rather transparent in a harmless sort of way.

HENRY. *(Laughing.)* I must admit his brain is called Mr. Zipper. I do apologize. I hope I haven't offended you.

VICTORIA. Not at all. *(Touches HENRY's arm and quickly pulls away.)* Good heavens, I'm feeling a little flustered... oh goodness, I haven't felt this way in years. I'm not sure what's come over me. Excuse me, I think I need to get a little air. *(Exits through nook French doors.)*

(Enter MRS. STANCLIFFE from the office, she pauses in the doorway, visible to the audience, but unnoticed by HENRY.)

HENRY. *(Pauses for a moment, picks up the manuscript page on which he has written Victoria's lines, holding that in his left hand, and the pansies held high in his right, faces down stage and drops to his right knee, to practice the speech and tries the following lines with the emphasis different each time.)* OH, my beautiful Buttercup...no, no, that's not right. Oh, my BEAUTIFUL Buttercup... no, no, no...OH MY BEAUTIFUL BUTTERCUP.

MRS. STANCLIFFE. *(Crosses L. towards HENRY.)* Good heavens Henry, what are you doing?

HENRY. *(Shuffles R. on his knees towards her and begins reading the paper.)* Oh, my beautiful Buttercup, when you look at me my heart skips a beat, and my passion knows no bounds. Whenever I see you I stop breathing. *(Pauses.)* Well, obviously I start again or I'd be dead. *(Reads from the paper again.)* I cannot stand the thought of us being apart one more moment. I must taste those ruby lips, feel the softness of your tender touch, I cannot live another moment without knowing you will be mine forever. *(Pauses, frowns, then turns the page over.)* Please, make me the happiest of men and say you will be my wife. *(Shoves the pansies at her.)*

MRS. STANCLIFFE. Taste my ruby red lips? *(Takes the pansies.)* Oh Henry... I don't know what to say. I don't under-stand....pansies....but it's not 5.05 on Saturday, *(Looks at her watch.)* it's 5.12 on Friday. *(Touches his forehead.)* Are you feeling ill my dear?

HENRY. *(Takes* **MRS. STANCLIFFE***'s hand and kisses it.)* I'm feeling wonderful…."My dear?" Would you mind if I got up?

MRS. STANCLIFFE. Here, let me help you. *(Assists Henry up.)*

HENRY. Well?

MRS. STANCLIFFE. Well what?

HENRY. About my proposal…

MRS. STANCLIFFE. My dear Henry, I really feel quite moved. I've never seen this side of you before. As a matter of fact, I've been feeling a little different myself since you left earlier this afternoon.

HENRY. Does this mean-?

MRS. STANCLIFFE. Perhaps.

HENRY. *(He grabs* **MRS. STANCLIFFE***'s hand and kisses it.)* This is exciting news my dear. *(Continues to kiss her hand.)*

(Enter **HILLARY** *from bedroom 2)*

MRS. STANCLIFFE. *(Quite flustered, now sees* **HILLARY** *and immediately withdraws her hand.)* Mr. Mitchell, I…um….I have a bed and breakfast to run and cannot stand here dilly dallying around. In precisely six minutes and forty-five seconds I must serve afternoon refreshments for my guests. Please excuse me. *(Exits to the kitchen.)*

HILLARY. *(Crosses R. to L. side of the couch.)* Hello Henry, it's good to see you again.

HENRY. *(Moves D. towards Hillary and gives her hug.)* It's good to see you too Hillary. Thanks for coming. Please, sit down.

HILLARY. *(Sits L. end of couch.)* I hope I wasn't interrupting anything.

HENRY. *(Sits in the chair.)* That's quite all right. As a matter of fact Mrs. Stancliffe is the reason I invited you here.

HILLARY. Now I'm really intrigued. We haven't worked together or seen each other since you retired several years ago. Then, all of a sudden, out of the blue, I get this phone call from you asking me to help you con-duct a field test on a pill that you say could change the lives of millions of women. You've told me all about this Venusia pill, and that I should make up a story about why I am here, but what does it have to do with Mrs. Stancliffe, and exactly how am I supposed to help you?

HENRY. For the past twenty years, I've been going nowhere fast with Mrs. Stancliffe. I adore her, and I want her to marry me, but she seems to have no romantic interest at all. If this pill works, maybe it will help arouse her romantic side again. I don't feel right about asking her to take the pill, until I've had at least one other test.

HILLARY. *(Pauses.)* You want me to be the guinea pig?

HENRY. Well, yes. But you do understand this is a totally natural product. It was made from a vegetable, and is absolutely safe for human consumption. I'd take it myself, but I'm not exactly right for the test.

HILLARY. And what makes you think I am?

HENRY. I thought of you because you are in the right age bracket, have an impartial scientific mind, and you're single.

HILLARY. Thanks Henry, you really know how to sweep a girl off her feet.

HENRY. Did I say something wrong?

HILLARY. No wonder Mrs. Stancliffe isn't succumbing to your charms. Henry, are you assuming I'm menopausal?

HENRY. You're not? Really? At your age?

HILLARY. Henry, be careful. Menopausal women have been known to eat their young. *(Laughs.)* However today you're safe, I took my crabby pill this morning.

HENRY. *(Laughs)* So, will you do it?

HILLARY. Why not, it might even be fun…if it works.

HENRY. All I ask is that you keep written notes on how you feel emotionally and physically. I'm not sure about the dosage. Why don't you try one now, and if nothing happens, take another in a couple of hours. *(Takes out the bottle of pills and hands them to her, then moves U.L. to the nook to pour her an iced tea.)*

HILLARY. *(Follows* **HENRY** *L. to the steps of the nook and takes out one pill.)* Henry, you've forgotten just one thing. If this is supposed to help a woman feel romantic, don't I need someone to feel romantic about?

HENRY. *(Moves to* **HILLARY** *and hands her the iced-tea.)* Ah, yes, …well …..there's Bud.

HILLARY. *(Takes the pill with a sip of the tea.)* Bud? You mean the Casanova with the molasses tongue? He's not exactly my type, *(She pauses and frowns a little.)* I think, but I guess I could record my feelings towards him, in the name of science of course.

HENRY. Perfect. If you do feel anything towards him, then it will only substantiate the effectiveness of the pill. I really do appreciate this Hillary. Oh, and by the way, Mrs. Stancliffe doesn't know anything about this, or the fact that I asked you to come here. We'll have to be careful not to let on. We can meet later and discuss your findings.

HILLARY. *(Hands Henry the glass.)* Don't worry Henry. I'll be discreet. Besides, I told her I was here to start meeting people socially again. I didn't know how close I was to the truth. *(Moves L. towards bedroom 2.)* I can't believe you talked me into this. Henry, you're going to owe me for this one. *(Exits into bedroom 2 and closes the door.)*

*(**HENRY** moves to the buffet and puts the glass down as* **CHARMAINE** *enters through the front door.* **CHARMAINE** *is age 55+, and a true southern belle, complete with femme fatale southern charm. Her libido is definitely working, and never stops. She is wearing an elegant, low cut summer dress, with matching purse and high-heeled shoes. She carries a small overnight case, which she puts down inside the front door.)*

CHARMAINE. *(Sees Henry.)* Well hi there handsome. Do y'all know where Mrs. Stancliffe is?

HENRY. *(Crosses R. to her.)* I believe she's in the kitchen. I expect she'll be out in a minute. I'm Henry Mitchell. *(Puts his hand out to shake hands.)*

CHARMAINE. *(Shakes his hand.)* Why hello Henry Mitchell, I'm Charmaine Beauregard. It's a pleasure to meet you. *(Looks around.)*

HENRY. The pleasure is all mine. Are you looking for something?

CHARMAINE. Not something, someone. You see, last year I met this charming gentleman from next door, and I had arranged for us to meet here.

HENRY. You mean Bud?

CHARMAINE. Oh, you know him? I just think he's the tom-cat's kitten.

HENRY. I'd agree with the tomcat.

CHARMAINE. Would you excuse me for a moment. *(Moves D.R. to the French doors and looks out.).*

HENRY. I'm sure he'll be here soon, while you're waiting, would you like some iced-tea?

CHARMAINE. Why, that's ever so nice. I'm as dry as an empty mint-julep glass on a hot summer afternoon.

HENRY. *(Moves U.S. to the buffet and pours a glass of iced-tea.)* Why don't you come and sit down.

CHARMAINE. *(Moves U.C. and sits in the chair.)* Do you work here, I don't remember seeing you here last year, but then, I rarely left my room.

HENRY. No, I live down the road. I'm what Mrs. Stancliffe calls, "Her Gentleman Caller."

CHARMAINE. My, my, a gentleman caller, how romantic.

HENRY. *(Moves D.S. and hands her the iced-tea, then sits on the couch L. side.)* That's the problem. There is no romance.

CHARMAINE. Excuse me?

HENRY. I'm sorry, I don't mean to trouble you with my problems.

CHARMAINE. Why I'm a great listener, and where romance is concerned, I'm like honey to a bee if you get my meaning.

HENRY. Thank you. That's very kind. If you don't mind,

Bud and I seem to be so different. Would you mind if I asked you a couple of questions?

CHARMAINE. That's O.K., but you know us southern gals don't kiss and tell.

HENRY. Of course, I was wondering why do "women of a certain age" find Bud attractive?

CHARMAINE. Well, I certainly don't know anything about "women of a certain age". For me, my Budly Studly knows how to make me feel all tingly inside. He's just so passionate.

HENRY. BUD?

CHARMAINE. Why that man's engine is always running.

HENRY. I can believe that, he does seem to have a "one track" mind.

CHARMAINE. My Budly has the gift of a silver tongue. He could charm the panties off my granny. Though why he'd want to I don't know. She's as ornery as a coon and fell out of the ugly tree, hitting every branch on the way down, bless her heart. *(BUD appears in the French doors and listens to the conversation, unseen by* HENRY *and* CHARMAINE.*)* Why, some men are all words and no action, but my Budly Studly is a pistol firing on all cylinders.

HENRY. BUD?

CHARMAINE. Why, he might not look it, but he is as strong as an ox, and has the stamina of a bull.

HENRY. BUD?

CHARMAINE. *(Fanning herself.)* Why, I'm feeling a little flushed just talking about him.

HENRY. BUD?

BUD. *(Enters through the D.S. French doors with wine and roses.)* Yes, Bud. For heaven's sake Henry, stop pestering this vision of loveliness. Never in my dreams have I seen such beauty, such charm, but the face in my dreams was never....

CHARMAINE. *(Runs over to* BUD *and throws her arms around him, practically knocking him over. She kisses him all over leaving large red lipstick marks on his face.)* Oh my Budly Studly, have I ever missed you. *(Takes the flowers and wine.)* Are these for little ol' me? You are such a sweetheart. *(Kisses him on the lips.).* I was afraid you'd forgotten me. *(Sticks a rose in* BUD*'s mouth.)* Now you just give me a few minutes to check in and freshen up, and then it'll be party time. *(Moves U.S. to the counter and rings the bell.)*

(Enter MRS. STANCLIFFE *from the kitchen carrying a tray of sandwiches, a bottle of wine, and wine glasses.)*

MRS. STANCLIFFE. *(Moves to the buffet.)* Welcome back Ms. Beauregard. I am sorry to keep you waiting. I will be with you in precisely 25 seconds. *(Arranges the wine and sandwiches.)*

CHARMAINE. That's quite all right. I have been wonderfully entertained by these two marvelous gentlemen.

MRS. STANCLIFFE. *(Crosses R to the counter.)* Mr. Davis, I know this establishment is called Rose Cottage, but if I wanted a statue of a man holding a rose in his mouth, I'd buy one.

BUD. *(Removes the rose from his mouth.)* Right Mrs. S. *(Moves to* CHARMAINE *and hands her the rose.)* You my dear are the rose *(Looks at* MRS. STANCLIFFE.*)* among thorns. *(Crosses L. and sits next to* HENRY.*)*

MRS. STANCLIFFE. *(Now behind the counter hands her a card.)* If you would just complete this, please. I hope you weren't bothered by those two.

CHARMAINE. I could never be bothered by my Budly Studly, and your gentleman caller is just a darlin.

MRS. STANCLIFFE. Henry?

CHARMAINE. If you don't mind my saying so, I think you two belong together, like love doves in a magnolia tree.

MRS. STANCLIFFE. Henry?

CHARMAINE. Why, he's as cute as a sack full of puppies.

MRS. STANCLIFFE. Henry?

CHARMAINE. I can tell you if I didn't have my Budly Studly *(Does a little finger wave to* **BUD**.*)* I'd be all over him like a chicken on a June bug.

*(***BUD** *finger waves back.)*

MRS. STANCLIFFE. Perhaps your Budly Studly….I mean… Mr. Davis would like to help you with your luggage. *(Rings bell.)* Mr. Davis, why don't you make yourself useful and help Ms. Beauregard to the Tahitian Sunset rose room. *(Exits to the office.)*

CHARMAINE. Really that's not necessary. *(Picks up her luggage and moves L.* **BUD** *comes D. behind the couch and attempts to take the suitcase.* **CHARMAINE** *links her arm in his, and still carrying the suitcase they cross L. to the door of bedroom 3.)* No, no sweetie pie, you're going to need all your strength for later. I'm just so anxious to be with you, but I do need a little time. Give me five minutes to slip into something more comfortable. *(Gives him a kiss on the lips, and exits into the bedroom, closing the door.)*

BUD. *(Sits in the R. chair.)* Panache Henry, it's all about panache.

HENRY. *(Comes D., sits on the sofa L. side.)* Maybe you're right about this panache stuff. Something is definitely different with Mrs. Stancliffe. She called me "my dear" earlier today.

BUD. Henry, I hate to burst your bubble, but I have a confession to make. I don't think it was your panache. I….um, "borrowed" some of your Venusia pills. I figured you wouldn't, so I ..well…I put one of them in a glass of iced-tea for Mrs. S.

HENRY. You what? What were you thinking.

BUD. Ah Henry, don't get mad, I was only trying to help you out, and it looks like I did.

HENRY. When did she drink it?

BUD. Well, actually I don't know, I left it on the buffet when Victoria came in.

HENRY. So we don't really know if she drank it or not.

BUD. Well, one of them did, because it's not there now.

(Enter **VICTORIA** *from the nook French doors, and comes D. behind the couch.)*

BUD. *(Stands and moves up to* **VICTORIA**.*) A*h, the beautiful butterfly returns. The strong arms that you have been longing for are here, awaiting you. *(Does a muscle man pose.)*

VICTORIA. You know, the last time I saw you I was promised roses, champagne and caviar. Are you all promises, or do you ever deliver?

BUD. Do I deliver? Does champagne have bubbles? I shall return in the twinkling of an eye. In five minutes you will have your champagne, your roses, your caviar and your Budly Studly.

VICTORIA. I shall be waiting for you in my room.

BUD. *(Looking at Charmaine's door.)* Ah, right, can we make that ten minutes? I need to replenish my …er…er… certain supplies. You shall not be disappointed ma cherie'. *(He starts to bow, then thinks better of it and blows a kiss instead, then exits through the R. French doors.)*

VICTORIA. *(Turns to* **HENRY**.*)* Hello again. How did the proposal go?

HENRY. She actually reacted quite differently, but now I'm not sure whether it was your words, or something else.

VICTORIA. Does it matter? She's changed. If I were writing this in one of my novels I might say, "Give into the passion that dwells within your breast. Do that which up till now you have been afraid to whisper." I know I am. Good evening Henry. *(Exits to bedroom 1.)*

CHARMAINE. *(Now wearing a short and sexy nightie, opens her door. She calls softly.)* Oh Bud….where are you my super sexy studly stallion?

HENRY. Bud?

CHARMAINE. I'm so sorry Mr. Mitchell. I have embarrassed myself. I thought I heard Bud's voice. I didn't realize y'all were still here. *(Quickly withdraws into her room leaving the door open.)*

(Enter Bud through the D.R. French doors with roses, champagne and caviar.)

BUD. *(Moves U.S to Victoria's door.)* Stayed to watch the master at work, eh Henry?

HENRY. *(Whispering,)* Bud, Bud. *(He signals to* **BUD** *that Charmaine's door is open.)*

CHARMAINE. *(Reappears at the door.)* BUDLY! Whatever are you doing? You wouldn't be two-timing me would you?

BUD. *(Turns quickly.)* I er…um…er….

HENRY. *(Strides R. and takes the flowers, champagne and caviar out of* **BUD***'s hands.)* He's just brought these for me to give to my true love, Buttercup.

BUD. Yeah, that's right,…. Buttercup?

HENRY. Yes Bud, Buttercup. *(Heads towards the front door, then turns.)* Now that's panache. Oh Buttercup, my beautiful Buttercup. *(Exits to front door.)*

CHARMAINE. Lets go Budly Studly. *(She retreats sexily into her room beckoning to Bud with her finger.* **BUD** *pops open a pill bottle and swallows one. Crosses L. to Charmaine's room and is about to enter when* **VICTORIA** *opens her door.)*

VICTORIA. *(Now wearing an elegant yet sensuous peignoir, strikes a pose in the doorway, and in a long, low raspy tone.)* Oh Bud!

*(***BUD** *in the entranceway of bedroom 3, quickly turns and sees* **VICTORIA**. *He glances back momentarily to Charmaine's room, then turns again and quickly crosses R. to* **VICTORIA**. *They embrace and exit into bedroom 1, closing the door.)*

MRS. STANCLIFFE. *(Enters from the office.)* Henry, is that you? *(Crosses L. and exits to the kitchen.)*

HENRY. *(Enters from the front door still carrying the champagne, caviar, and flowers.)* Oh Buttercup, where are you? I have a surprise for you. *(Exits to the office.)*

MRS. STANCLIFFE. *(Re-enters from the kitchen.)* Henry? This is most vexing. I have been looking for you for precisely forty-three and one half seconds. *(Exits to the front door.)*

*(***HENRY**, *re-enters from the office, still carrying the champagne, caviar and flowers. He pauses by the front desk, as* **BUD**, *now somewhat disheveled, staggers out of*

B.R.1, closes the door, crosses L. and leans on the back of the couch as he pops a pill, watched by **HENRY**.*)*

CHARMAINE. *(Strikes a pose in the doorway of BR 3.)* Why Budly, don't you know it's not nice to keep a lady waitin'?

*(***BUD*** glances R. at B.R. 1, then crosses L. as* **CHAR-MAINE** *grabs him and drags him into bedroom 3, closing the door. There are noises off in B.R. 3, giggling and shrieking from* **CHARMAINE** *as* **HENRY** *listens.)*

HENRY. *(Stands for a moment, looks in amazement at the door of bedroom 1, then bedroom 3.)* I give up Buttercup, I'm going home. *(Places the champagne, flowers and caviar on the coffee table, and exits nook French doors.)*

VICTORIA. *(Enters from B.R.1)* Bud, where did you get to? *(Sees the flowers, crosses to the coffee table, picks up the card and reads.)* "Champagne, roses and caviar, for such a vision of loveliness, such beauty, such charm. I have dreamed about you many times in the past year, but the face in my dreams was never as beautiful as the one that will be in my arms tonight." Oh how sweet. Budly, come out, come out where ever you are, I'll be waiting for you. *(Takes the flowers, champagne, and caviar, and exits to B.R. 1, leaving the door open.)*

*(***BUD***, staggers out of bedroom 3. He is now is a state of disarray. His shirt is unbuttoned and hanging out of his pants, he has no shoes and only one sock. He staggers R. to the L. end of the couch and pops one more pill. He looks at the door of bedroom 1, then bedroom 3. He takes a step towards bedroom 1, stops, turns and takes a step towards bedroom 3, as the door to BR 2 slowly opens and* **HILLARY** *appears dressed in sensuous lounge wear. She beckons to* **BUD**. *He looks at B.R 3, then at B.R. 1, then at* **HILLARY**, *and finally, with a loud moan, collapses on the couch.)*

CURTAIN

ACT II

The following day, at precisely 4:37 post meridian.

The curtain rises on an empty set. After a moment or two, **BUD DAVIS** *appears in the D.R. French doors, dressed in Khaki pants, sport shirt with collar and suspenders. He now leans on a walker, which he carefully hides outside the window. He looks around, and seeing no one, moves towards the reservation desk and begins to search through the computer.*

Enter **MRS. STANCLIFFE** *from the nook French doors, with a basket of fresh cut flowers from the garden and a pair of scissors. She is dressed in much the same manner as yesterday, but her dress today has a little color.*

MRS. STANCLIFFE. *(Quickly crosses R.)* Mr. Bud Davis, just exactly what do you think you are doing?

BUD. What does it look like I'm doing? It's what I do every afternoon, checking the reservations to see if any of my "chicks" are arriving today.

MRS. STANCLIFFE. *(Now at the counter, closes the computer, almost on Bud's fingers.)* I have told you repeatedly, there are no "chicks". This is a respectable bed & breakfast.

BUD. I know that, these are respectable chicks.

MRS. STANCLIFFE. For your information, there are no new "chicks", as you so rudely call them, checking in today.

BUD. Oh come on now Mrs. S. remember, Confucius said, "He who checks the chicks in, gets to check the chicks out."

MRS. STANCLIFFE. Confucius never said that.

BUD. Well, he should have, he'd have picked up more chicks.

MRS. STANCLIFFE. I shall ignore that. However, before I

send you on your way, I wish to have words with you regarding Ms. Ambrose.

BUD. Alright Mrs. S, let me just get some iced-tea. *(Wanders U.L. to the buffet, and pours himself a glass.)*

MRS. STANCLIFFE. I do not want her to be pestered by you. As you know, she's a highly renowned writer of romance novels, but what you probably don't know is she is here on business.

BUD. *(At the buffet, with his back to* **MRS. STANCLIFFE** *and almost to himself.)* And what you don't know is her business is writing about Bud the Stud

MRS. STANCLIFFE. *(Doesn't hear* **BUD** *'s last remark.)* She is on a timeline, and is having difficulty completing her latest novel.

BUD. Writers block, huh?

MRS. STANCLIFFE. Not at all, she has written so many novels, that she is having difficulty knowing how this one will progress. She wants this one to be true to life, and is trying to find a creative way for the heroine to reconcile herself with her lover, bringing everything to a romantic conclusion.

BUD. I can certainly be of assistance with that. I am, after all, a romance aficionado. Have no fear Mrs. S., I won't pester her, but I will definitely give her what she needs to find the ultimate romantic experience.

MRS. STANCLIFFE. Why Bud, that's exactly the kind of help she needs.

BUD. After all, last year, in the throes of passion, I did get her name right.

MRS. STANCLIFFE. Mr. Davis, I do not wish to know anything about your "throes." I have told her that she will have all the peace and quiet she needs to complete her romance.

BUD. So she's here to continue where she left off?

MRS. STANCLIFFE. Absolutely. *(Bud reacts.)* I am counting on you to cooperate, so that she can find the perfect ending for "The Summer Cottage, My Journey of Love".

BUD. Bud the Stud to the rescue. Neither snow, nor rain, nor heat, nor gloom of night, shall keep me from my appointed rounds.

MRS. STANCLIFFE. Didn't that used to be the motto of the US postal service?

BUD. Yes, …but I deliver.

MRS. STANCLIFFE. But do you deliver on Sundays, Christmas, New Years, Easter, President's Day, Memorial Day, Martin Luther King Day, Independence Day, Labor Day, Thanksgiving….

BUD. *(Interrupting.)* Good one Mrs. S. Let's just leave it that I'm your man, and you can count on me. Bud the Stud will guarantee first class, same day delivery. Which reminds me, with three chicks already on the go, I need to go check on my supply of condoms.

MRS. STANCLIFFE. I find this conversation very distasteful, and in the hopes that you will remove yourself from these premises, am terminating it at precisely 4:41 post meridian. Good day Mr. Davis.

*(Enter **VICTORIA** from B.R. 1, now wearing a blouse and pants.)*

VICTORIA. Good afternoon, I'm just taking a little breather, and thought I'd get a glass of iced tea. *(She moves U.L. towards the breakfast nook.)*

MRS. STANCLIFFE. Please, help yourself. How is it going?

VICTORIA. I'm still struggling, but I think I see some light at the end of the tunnel.

MRS. STANCLIFFE. *(To **BUD**.)* Now, you promised to help, and I'm going to hold you to your word. I expect you to be on your best behavior. Ms. Ambrose, please excuse me, I have to attend to these flowers. I leave you in Mr. Davis's capable hands. *(Exits to the office with the basket of flowers.)*

BUD. *(Holding his hands out, as if cupping a woman's breasts.)* R-I-I-I-IGHT!

VICTORIA. *(Now at the buffet pouring her tea.)* Mr. Davis, I think perhaps I need to explain my behavior last night.

BUD. No explanation is necessary. I now understand why you are here.

VICTORIA. *(Moves D.S to the couch and sits L.)* Oh, I'm so glad you do.

BUD. *(Sits on the couch R.)* Mrs. Stancliffe tells me that I can help you.

VICTORIA. Really?

BUD. Of course, I have a lot of experience in this area.

VICTORIA. Then you've read my work?

BUD. I have.

VICTORIA. Well, Ok, if you're sure you don't mind, by all means let's do it together. *(BUD reacts.)* My problem is I need to bring the two lovers together again after all those misunderstandings.

BUD. Champagne, moonlight and whispers of love might solve the problem.

VICTORIA. I've done that before, too mundane this time.

BUD. *(Reacts.)* Really?

VICTORIA. Yes, I need something new, something exciting, something extraordinary.

BUD. You mean that? Something new, exciting, extraordinary?

VICTORIA. Yes, of course.

BUD. O.K. What do you have in mind?

VICTORIA. I'm not sure. You said you might be able to help. How do you think we should do it?

BUD. Well, just exactly how innovative do you want to be?

VICTORIA. I'd like to find passion beyond my wildest dreams.

BUD. Right. Wildest dreams? We can handle that. Where?

VICTORIA. Well obviously, it has to be in the cottage of love.

BUD. Right. When?

VICTORIA. I need to do it now, right away, tonight if possible.

BUD. It's definitely possible.

VICTORIA. But remember, it must be new and different, or it simply won't work for me.

BUD. Right. I'm your man.

VICTORIA. Maybe we can do it with just words?

BUD. No, that won't work at all. There's got to be action.

VICTORIA. Suppose one of them confesses to the other.

BUD. What about?

VICTORIA. Well, you know, past indiscretions.

BUD. You think that would do it?

VICTORIA. It might.

BUD. But that's not passion beyond your wildest dreams.

VICTORIA. Oh, that always follows a confession.

BUD. Then I confess. *(Moves closer and starts to kiss her arm.)* Don't worry about our misunderstanding. Just remember our night of passion in "The Cottage Of Love". I am your Adonis, the man of your dreams, the man who will…

VICTORIA. Be singing a high "C" if he doesn't control himself.

BUD. *(Releases her arm.)* I'm only bringing the two lovers together.

VICTORIA. *(Starts to laugh.)* Oh my goodness, you mean you thought that we… that you and I…. that I was writing about you? We've never been together.

BUD. We haven't?

VICTORIA. Absolutely not. Sorry to burst your bubble Bud, but I need to get back to my writing. *(Exits to B.R. 1)*

BUD. *(Totally deflated.)* Oh…Oh well, I'm down from three chicks to two…better go check on my supply of condoms.

(BUD exits through the D.R. French doors, as MRS. STANCLIFFE enters through the office, and as HENRY enters through the nook French doors. He is dressed as yesterday, with a different color polo shirt. He carries a huge bouquet of assorted flowers, so large his face is barely visible behind them. He crosses R. and begins the "Victoria" proposal, leaning around the flowers.)

HENRY. Oh, my beautiful Buttercup, when you look at me my heart skips a beat, and my passion knows no bounds. Whenever I see you I stop breathing. I cannot stand the thought of us being apart one more moment. I must taste those ruby lips, er...um...*(At this point he forgets the lines, and hiding behind the flowers, unseen by* **MRS. STANCLIFFE,** *he quickly takes a piece of paper from his pocket and continues reading.)* er...feel the softness of your tender touch, I cannot live another moment without knowing you will be mine forever. *(Drops to his knees and shoves the flowers towards her.)* Please, make me the happiest of men and say you will be my wife.

MRS. STANCLIFFE. *(Takes the flowers.)* Henry dear, please get up. You're going to hurt your knees. *(***HENRY** *stands up.)* I know we had today's pansies yesterday, and again you surprise me. These are lovely Henry. Are you trying to sweep me off my feet?

HENRY. Yes, I mean no, I mean....do you want me to?

MRS. STANCLIFFE. *(Moves R. and puts the flowers on the counter.)* Henry, I don't know what got into me yesterday, but I...

HENRY. I'm afraid I do know what got into you.

MRS. STANCLIFFE. I beg your pardon?

HENRY. I have a confession to make. Please come and sit down. *(They come D.,* **MRS. STANCLIFFE** *sits in the R. chair,* **HENRY** *sits on the couch L. side.)* Would you like the long version or the short version?

MRS. STANCLIFFE. *(Looks at her watch.)* I can spare you precisely one and three-quarter minutes.

HENRY. I have been working in my lab on a pill to enhance the libido of menopausal women. It is called Venusia. Unfortunately Bud inadvertently got his hands on some of them and put one in a glass of iced-tea yesterday, which he left on the buffet, and which you may have drunk.

MRS. STANCLIFFE. May have drunk?

HENRY. We're not sure whether you drank it or Ms.

Ambrose. I can assure you the pill is made from a vegetable, is perfectly harmless, and may or may not work. It was never my intention for anybody to take the pill unknowingly, especially you my dear.

MRS. STANCLIFFE. Thank you for telling me Henry, I appreciate that. I am not at all pleased that I was in any way involved in this unfortunate situation, but, since Ms. Ambrose was also involved, I insist that you also tell her what has occurred. *(Crosses to bedroom 1, and knocks on the door.* **VICTORIA,** *opens the door and steps into the room as* **HENRY** *stands.)* I am so sorry to disturb you, but Henry, I mean, Mr. Mitchell needs to speak with you. *(She picks up the flowers, then crosses L. behind the couch, pauses, and says to* **HENRY.)** Venusia? Henry, you are full of surprises. *(Exits to the kitchen.)*

HENRY. I hope we didn't disturb you.

VICTORIA. *(Crosses L. to the chair and sits.)* Actually, I was just about to take a break.

HENRY. *(Sits.)* Ms. Ambrose, I'm afraid I have something to tell you, which may upset you.

VICTORIA. Please, call me Victoria. This does sound ominous. Smile Henry, I promise not to bite.

HENRY. First off, I want to thank you again for all your help with Mrs. Stancliffe, things were going better, until my confession, which leads me now to you.

VICTORIA. Confession Henry? I'm all ears.

HENRY. In my lab at home I have developed a pill called Venusia, which is intended to increase the libido in menopausal women. Yesterday, unknown to me, Mr. Davis placed one of those pills in an iced-tea, which he intended Mrs. Stancliffe to drink. The problem was your arrival.

VICTORIA. Thanks Henry.

HENRY. No, no, what I mean is, when you arrived, Bud left the drink on the buffet, and apparently, either you or Mrs. Stancliffe drank it.

VICTORIA. *(Breaks into tears.)* Oh no!

HENRY. Oh please, don't cry. The pill is all natural, made from plant extract, it can't hurt you, I don't even know if it works.

VICTORIA. *(Still crying.)* It's not that, it's just that, well yesterday, I felt something I haven't felt in years. I was so excited to find out that I still had these feelings, and now, I discover it might have been this pill.

HENRY. *(Hands her a handkerchief.)* Please, stop crying. I don't do well with crying women.

VICTORIA. *(Now becomes angry.)* You don't do well with crying women? It's always about men, you don't even care that I might have taken this pill, or that I don't have feelings. Sex, that's all you men ever think about.

HENRY. Ms. Ambrose I really am terribly sorry. I didn't mean to upset you, I really do care, and I find you very attractive and personable.

VICTORIA. You do? *(Starts to weep again.)* Oh, I'm so sorry, thank you. I don't know what's wrong with me. It seems these days that my hormones are in charge, and my mind is just along for the ride. *(Blows a loud raspberry into the handkerchief and tries to hand it back to **HENRY**.)*

HENRY. *(Pauses, looks at the handkerchief.)* Why don't you keep it. *(Enter **CHARMAINE** from bedroom 3. She is wearing an attractive, low cut sundress and high-heeled sandals. **HENRY** leaps to his feet.)* Ms. Beauregard, I'm so glad you're here, Ms. Ambrose seems to be a little upset. I wonder if you could lend a hand.

CHARMAINE. *(Crosses to behind the L. chair and places her hand on **VICTORIA**'S shoulder.)* Honey, are those tears? Why my granny used to tell me that tears are nothing but the nectar of the soul, pouring forth upon the earth.

HENRY. It looks like you're in capable hands Ms. Ambrose, if you'll excuse me, I'll see the both of you later. *(Exits through the nook French doors leaving them open.)*

VICTORIA. Thank you. I just can't seem to stop crying.

CHARMAINE. *(Sits R. on the couch.)* Now why don't you tell me what those tears are all about.

VICTORIA. *(Still sobbing.)* I really don't know. These days it doesn't take very much for me to cry.

CHARMAINE. Well, my granny always said, "No use cryin' a river of tears, 'less you have something to be cryin' about."

VICTORIA. *(Sniffling)* Well, I'm a writer of romance novels, I have a deadline to meet and I don't seem to be able to find the right words anymore.

CHARMAINE. You mean you got writer's block?

VICTORIA. I guess so.

CHARMAINE. Is it the words you can't find, or the romance to write about?

VICTORIA. I think it's a little of both.

CHARMAINE. Well honey, turn that frown upside down, it's your lucky day. Charmaine Beauregard to the rescue.

VICTORIA. What do you mean?

CHARMAINE. Honey, I can't give you the words, but I sure can give you stuff to write about.

VICTORIA. Really?

CHARMAINE. Why when my Budly Studly and I meet up again this evening, you just take notes, and I'll give you meat for the bones of your next book. I always wanted to be a leadin' lady in a romance novel.

VICTORIA. *(Bursts into tears again.)* Me too!

CHARMAINE. Now, now honey child, you got more tears than a magnolia tree has blossoms in the springtime. We can't all be leadin' ladies.

VICTORIA. I know, but yesterday, well….I thought just maybe, my body hadn't given up the ghost, that I still had what it took, that there was still some sizzle left inside me, that -

CHARMAINE. Whatever are you talkin' about?

VICTORIA. Well, it seems that on top of all the problems with my writing, I may have taken a pill which is supposed to help menopausal women with their libido, and that may have been why I succumbed to Mr. Davis' charms. *(Begins to wail.)*

CHARMAINE. What? Mr. Davis? Succumbed?

VICTORIA. *(Sniffling.)* Well, nothing happened, but I did invite him into my room.

CHARMAINE. Did he accept the invitation?

VICTORIA. Well, yes

CHARMAINE. Well, if that don't put pepper in the gumbo. He's nothing but a two-timing tomcat.

VICTORIA. You mean, he was with you too? *(Starts to cry)*

CHARMAINE. Yes, but nothing happened, and now I know why. *(Starts to cry.)* My Budly Studly, how could you do this to me? I didn't expect you to be faithful, but not in the same house, on the same day, at the same time. *(Weeping loudly now.)*

VICTORIA. Men. *(Weeping loudly, blows another raspberry.)*

(Enter MRS. STANCLIFFE from the kitchen. She quickly closes the nook French doors.)

MRS. STANCLIFFE. It's got quite chilly in here. Why can't you ever have a good hot flash when you need one?

(VICTORIA & CHARMAINE in unison give a loud wail)

In heaven's name, what is going on? *(Comes D. L. of the couch.)*

VICTORIA & CHARMAINE. BUD!

MRS. STANCLIFFE. *(Sits on the couch L. end.)* What has that little weasel been up to now?

CHARMAINE. My Budly Studly was dilly-dallying with both of us.

VICTORIA. At the same time.

CHARMAINE. My Budly Dudly Do-Right done me wrong.

(CHARMAINE & VICTORIA begin to weep and wail again.)

MRS. STANCLIFFE. *(Looks first at CHARMAINE, then at VICTORIA.)* Oohh, that little....that lower than a snakes belly....how dare he? Wanting me to take that pill... Oh my bed & breakfast....what's to become of its reputation with that little skunk around. *(She starts to weep *and the noise brings* **HILLARY** *out of bedroom 2. She is now wearing a summer skirt, matching top and sandals.)*

HILLARY Why are you all weeping? *(Crosses R. to the L. end of the couch.)*

CHARMAINE}

VICTORIA} BUD!

MRS. STANCLIFFE}

HILLARY. What about Bud?

*(**HILLARY**, **CHARMAINE**, and **VICTORIA** all try to talk at once.)*

HILLARY. Whoa, one at a time.

CHARMAINE. He has two-timed me.

VICTORIA. …and I'm the two-timer he two-timed with.

MRS. STANCLIFFE. …and it's all because of a pill that Bud gave us.

HILLARY. What pill?

MRS. STANCLIFFE. It's supposed to increase the libido in menopausal women and it's called….

HILLARY. Venusia.

*(There is a long pause as **CHARMAINE**, **MRS. STAN-CLIFFE**, and **VICTORIA** stare at **HILLARY**.)*

VICTORIA. How do you know what it's called?

HILLARY. Ladies, I'm afraid it's time for me to confess. I am an old friend of Mr. Mitchell's, and I used to work with him. He called me and asked me to be the guinea pig and try out the Venusia pills. I agreed in the name of science. What I don't understand is how Bud got his hands on them. I thought Henry had given them all to me. Oh, and by the way, I'm afraid it's three-timing.

CHARMAINE. You too?

HILLARY. Well nothing happened, but it could have.

CHARMAINE. Why that weasel was busier than a one-legged man at a butt kicking contest.

VICTORIA. So the pill actually works?

HILLARY. The results are not yet conclusive. We really can't be sure.

CHARMAINE. I didn't take a pill. Maybe it really is "Bud the Stud."

MRS. STANCLIFFE. Either way, he needs to be taught a lesson.

CHARMAINE. I agree, why, he thinks the sun comes up just to hear him crow. That rooster needs to come down off his henhouse roof.

VICTORIA. In all my novels, I have never imagined a scum as deceitful as Bud.

HILLARY. Wait a minute everyone. Didn't we all succumb to his charms? I know I did.

MRS. STANCLIFFE. Be that as it may, what Bud did was wrong.

CHARMAINE. May I see the pills?

HILLARY. Sure, I'll go get them. *(Exits to bedroom 2.)*

CHARMAINE. I of course don't ever need pills like that, but if they really do work, it can't hurt.

MRS. STANCLIFFE. You know, I did feel a little different yesterday.

VICTORIA. Me too.

HILLARY. *(Enters from bedroom 2 with the pill bottle and crosses behind the couch and hands the pills to* **CHARMAINE** *who opens the bottle.)* Here you are.

CHARMAINE. Why these little blue pills look just like those Viagra pills that Bud seems to live on.

MRS. STANCLIFFE. That's it! That's how we fix Bud the Stud.

VICTORIA. What do you mean?

MRS. STANCLIFFE. We'll swap Bud's Viagra with the Venusia. He won't know the difference, and Bud the Stud, will become Bud the Dud.

VICTORIA. How do we get Bud's pills away from him?

CHARMAINE. Leave it to me. His ass is grass and I'm the lawnmower. *(***BUD** *appears outside the D.R. French doors, just visible to the audience, but not to anyone on stage. He stops and listens.)* I'm sure I can get him into my room and ready for action.

(BUD reacts enthusiastically.)

VICTORIA. I can do that too.

(BUD reacts enthusiastically.)

HILLARY. I'll be the back-up.

(BUD reacts enthusiastically.)

MRS. STANCLIFFE. I wouldn't mind being in on this as well.

(BUD reacts unenthusiastically and hurriedly leaves.)

HILLARY. *(Moves U. to the buffet.)* OK, I'll just leave the Venusia pills here, and whoever gets Bud's Viagra can swap them. *(Places the pill bottle on the buffet.)*

CHARMAINE. Ladies, believe me when a man thinks he's going to the Promised Land, his engine is running, but ain't nobody driving. I'll have no problem getting those pills from Bud. Victoria, you stand by, I'll make sure he leaves them out here, and then I'll get him into my room. That's when you can make the switch.

MRS. STANCLIFFE. It is now precisely 4:48 p.m., and if I have calculated correctly, Bud will be creeping back in here any minute.

HILLARY. O.K., everybody, stand by in your rooms.

MRS. STANCLIFFE. I'll be in my office. *(Exits to office.)*

(VICTORIA exits to bedroom 1, HILLARY exits to bedroom 2, CHARMAINE exits to bedroom 3. There is a brief pause. MRS. STANCLIFEE enters from the office, looks furtively around, quickly crosses L. to the buffet, swallows a Venusia pill, and quickly returns to the office. HILLARY enters from bedroom 2, looks furtively around, moves U. to the buffet, swallows a Venusia pill and returns to bedroom 2 closing the door. VICTORIA enters from bedroom 1, looks furtively around, crosses quickly to the buffet, swallows a Venusia pill, and returns to bedroom 1 leaving the door slightly ajar. CHARMAINE enters from bedroom 3, looks furtively around, goes up to the buffet, swallows a Venusia pill, and returns quickly to bedroom 3, leaving the door open. Enter BUD from the D.R. French doors.)

CHARMAINE. *(Enters from bedroom 3, crosses quickly R. flings her arms around* **BUD**'*s neck and kisses him full on the lips.)* Take me now my Budly Studly. *(She pulls him backwards towards the couch, turns him around, pushes him on his back on the couch with his head R. and feet L., then falls on top of him.)*

BUD. Now?

CHARMAINE. What's wrong with now?

BUD. Well, I'm…I'm….I'm not sure I'm ready.

CHARMAINE. *(Kisses him passionately again, as* **BUD** *fumbles in his pants pocket with his right hand for the pill bottle. He finally takes it out, seen by the audience.* **CHARMAINE** *sees the bottle, and takes it from him.)* Why Budly, whatever are you doing? These aren't what I think they are, are they? Why someone as big and strong as you doesn't need to take a little blue pill? *(Kisses him again.)* Come on lover boy, lets go to my room. *(She stands up and places the pill bottle on the small table, gives an O.K. sign to* **VICTORIA**'*s door, then pulls* **BUD** *off the couch and into bedroom 3, leaving it slightly ajar.)*

VICTORIA. *(Immediately rushes in from bedroom 1, runs over to the buffet, picks up the Venusia bottle, crosses back R. and puts it on the small table. She picks up the Viagra bottle, crosses to bedroom 2, and knocks on the door.* **HILLARY** *opens the door.)* We've made the switch. *(She hands* **HILLARY** *the Viagra bottle and they give each other a high five.)*

(Immediately, **BUD**, *now disheveled, runs out of bedroom 3, as* **VICTORIA** *and* **HILLARY**, *still visible to the audience, back off in the doorway a little and watch.* **BUD**, *crosses to the small table, takes a pill, takes two or three steps towards bedroom 3, stops, looks back at the pill bottle, rushes back, pops a second pill, and quickly exits into bedroom 3 closing the door. Enter* **HENRY** *from the nook French doors carrying a huge teddy bear.)*

VICTORIA. It's Henry, I need to talk to him. *(Crosses R.)*

HILLARY. Cute Mr. Mitchell, I can barely see you. *(Exits to B.R. 2, closing the door.)*

VICTORIA. Henry, I'm so glad you're back. I just want to apologize, I feel so foolish, breaking down and crying like that. I think I'm just menopausally challenged today.

HENRY. Don't worry about it.

VICTORIA. A bear Henry? Nice touch. It must be going well.

HENRY. Well, it certainly was going better, thanks to your coaching, but since this Venusia mix-up, I think I'm on shaky ground, so I bought the bear and wrote some words to go with it. As long as you're here, would you mind if I practiced them on you?

VICTORIA. Not at all Henry.

HENRY. Please, sit down. (**HENRY** *sits couch L. side and puts the bear on the couch R. side.* **VICTORIA** *sits in the chair.* **HENRY** *takes a piece of paper out of his pocket and reads.*) "Oh, my beautiful Buttercup, I have bought you this bear because it reminds me of your beauty. You are not hairy like this bear, but you have beautiful hair. Bears like to eat honey and I want you to be my honey. Bears are warm and cuddly, and I think you are too. Bears are beautiful, and so are you. I do not want to marry this bear, but I want to marry you". So, what do you think?

VICTORIA. I'm sure you are a brilliant scientist.

HENRY. No good huh?

VICTORIA. It's very -er-um- different Henry. Maybe we can punch it up a bit? Let me jot something down for you. (**HENRY** *hands her his paper and a pencil from his pocket.* **VICTORIA** *writes.*)

HENRY. I really do appreciate this. I guess you can tell I'm not a writer.

VICTORIA. (*Busy writing.*) We can't all be good at everything, I seem to be all words, but no action.

HENRY. It's better than me, no words and no action.

VICTORIA. Well, maybe this will help. (*Hands* **HENRY** *the paper and pencil.*)

HENRY. *(Reading.)* Oh, wow, ...oh...this is terrific. Can I practice?

VICTORIA. *(Laughing.)* Spontaneity is not your middle name, is it Henry. Alright, let's hear it.

(Enter MRS. STANCLIFFE from the kitchen carrying a tray of sandwiches and a bottle of wine. She places the tray on the table and sees HENRY come D. and drop to one knee in front of VICTORIA. MRS. STANCLIFFE quickly steps back in the archway, just visible to the audience.)

HENRY. *(Reading the paper, which is not visible to MRS. STAN-CLIFFE.)* Please accept this bear as a symbol of my love for you. Your hair glistening in the moonlight, out-shines the stars themselves. I can only imagine that your kiss tastes like the nectar of the gods, sweeter than honey itself. The dream of cuddling you on a cold winter's night brings warmth to my heart and fire to my loins. *(MRS. STANCLIFFE reacts.)* Share my love, my life, my bed; you are like the face that launched a thousand ships, marry me my Helen of Troy.

MRS. STANCLIFFE. *(Comes D.)* Henry, how could you?

HENRY. *(Stands.)* How could I what?

MRS. STANCLIFFE. Propose to Ms. Ambrose, you hardly know her.

VICTORIA. *(Laughing.)* Henry, I think we found the right words. Mrs. Stancliffe, the proposal was for you, Henry was nervous, he wanted to make it perfect for you, so he was simply practicing. Oh how I wish I had a man like Henry in my life. How lucky you are Mrs. Stancliffe. Good luck Henry. *(Exits to BR. 1 and closes the door.)*

MRS. STANCLIFFE. Oh Henry dear, were those words really for me?

HENRY. Yes my love.

MRS. STANCLIFFE. I don't know what to say.

HENRY. You could say yes.

MRS. STANCLIFFE. Henry, I'm going to change into something a little more comfortable, and when I return in precisely 10 and ¾ minutes, I would love to listen to you and that beautiful proposal.

HENRY. You mean you might....I mean....is it possible? Oh Buttercup!

MRS. STANCLIFFE. *(Gives* **HENRY** *a peck on the cheek, goes U.S. to the office door, stops, turns.)* Fire in your loins, Henry? *(Fanning herself.)* Oh goodness!

(Exits to the office.)

(HENRY *picks up the bear and begins to waltz around the room with it singing softly to himself.)*

BUD. *(In the doorway of BR.3, now somewhat disheveled, with one of his shirt-tails outside his pants, partially unbuttoned.)* Hold that thought, don't go away, give me a few minutes, your Budly Studly will be back. *(Closes the door. Clearly upset he rushes to the table, and takes another pill.)* What is wrong with these stupid pills? I've never had this trouble before. *(Starts to fan himself.)* And why am I so hot?

HENRY. And cranky too. You're beginning to sound just like all the women around here.

BUD. *(Starts to weep.)* What's happening to me. Nothings working, I've got hot flashes one minute, and the next I could weep at the drop of a hat.

HENRY. And don't forget cranky. Bud, if you were a woman I'd say you were menopausal.

BUD. *(Takes another pill.)* They just need a little more time to take effect. *(Notices the bear.)* Who's your friend Henry?

HENRY. *(Puts the bear down and moves L.)* Never mind the bear Bud. Listen, I think Mrs. Stancliffe is about to accept my proposal, but I'm a little nervous now because she's expecting fire in my loins.

BUD. Fire in your loins?

HENRY. Yes, but it's been such a long time, I'm afraid there might not be any fire left in my loins.

BUD. No problem Henry. *(Opens the pill bottle and hands him a pill.)* Take one of these, I hope they're not a bad batch. They seem to be taking forever to work today. So you'd better take two, *(Hands him another pill.)* That should put some fire in your loins. *(Looks into bottle, then turns upside down to show it's empty.)*

HENRY. O.K., I will, pass me a drink.

BUD. *(Comes D. and hands HENRY a drink.)* Enjoy my boy. Looks like I'm out of my happy pills, I need to replenish my supplies. If Charmaine is looking for me, tell her I'll be right back. *(Exit D.R. French doors.)*

HENRY. *(Looks at the pills in his hand and looks furtively around.)* Ah, what the heck. *(Swallows pills.)*

CHARMAINE. *(Enters from B.R. 3)* Oh Budly, whatever is keeping you? Why Henry, how nice to see you.

HENRY. If you're looking for Bud, he stepped out for a moment, but he said to tell you he'd be right back.

CHARMAINE. *(Laughing, she crosses R to Victoria's door and knocks.)* It won't surprise me if that two-timing hound dog never comes back, and that Henry, would suit me just fine. *(VICTORIA appears in the doorway.)* Operation "Bud the Dud" worked like a charm, and that leaves me hotter than that proverbial cat on a tin roof. So, grab your pencil and watch your leadin' lady in action. *(Turns to HENRY.)* Now, honey lamb, why don't you come and sit next to little ol' Charmaine on the couch.

(She sits couch R. side, as HENRY sits on the couch L. side. VICTORIA disappears momentarily, and immediately reappears in the doorway, with a pad and pencil, where she stays visible to the audience, but not to HENRY.)

HENRY. It sounds like you're upset with Bud.

CHARMAINE. I don't really want to talk about that little weasel, I really want to talk about us.

HENRY. Us?

CHARMAINE. Yes Henry us. *(Runs her fingers through his hair.)* Ever since I saw you I wanted you. *(*Freeze.)*

VICTORIA. *(Facing D.S. to the audience.)* Her quivering lips parted as she leaned towards him, placing her sylph like hands on the corded steel muscles of his arm. As she gazed into his eyes she realized at that moment that she must have her handsome Henry. She dreamt of nothing else, but to ravish him in the moonlight.

HENRY. But, I have Mrs. Stancliffe. *(*Freeze)*

VICTORIA. He was promised to another, and would not succumb to the temptation before him, no matter how beautiful and sensuous she was.

CHARMAINE. *(Sticks her chest out.)* Don't you find me attractive, Henry? *(*Freeze)*

VICTORIA. Her glistening bosom thrust forward as she whispered into the night, "Am I too voluptuous for you? Don't you feel the passion in your heart? Can't you feel the desire for me welling up inside you?"

HENRY. Well, of course, I think you're a beautiful woman. *(*Freeze)*

VICTORIA. Her hair was glistening like moonlight upon a shimmering lake, her eyes were pools of liquid amber, her body was full of mystery and longing that would excite any man.

HENRY. *(Starts to fan himself and tap his right foot again.)* Excuse me, I don't know what's wrong with me, I'm feeling quite flushed.

CHARMAINE. Why Henry, it's nothing to worry about. All my men get hot under the collar when I turn up the heat.

HENRY. *(Bursts into tears.)* Oh dear, I've never felt like this before.

VICTORIA. I can't write this, romance novel heroes don't cry.

HENRY. Excuse me, I've got to get some air for a moment. *(Moves up to the nook French doors, opens them and stands there fanning himself, then steps outside, as* **VICTORIA** *crosses L. to* **CHARMAINE.**)*

VICTORIA. Is he all right?

CHARMAINE. I'm not sure, he's acting very strangely. If he was a woman, I'd say he was having hot flashes. I don't seem to be getting anywhere with him, but did I give you anything to write about?

VICTORIA. Oh yes, you were great. I can't wait to get writing. By the way, does Hillary know that operation "Bud the Dud" is a success?

CHARMAINE. No, we'd better let her know.

VICTORIA. You tell her, I need to get writing. *(Returns R. to B.R. 1 and closes the door as* **CHARMAINE** *crosses L. to B.R. 2 and knocks on the door, which* **HILLARY** *opens.)*

CHARMAINE. It worked. Bud the Stud is now Bud the Dud and he's feeling lower than a toad in a dry well.

HILLARY. So where is he?

CHARMAINE. I don't know. He ran out of my room like a hound dog with his tail between his legs and said he'd be back. I haven't seen him since. What I am concerned about is Henry.

HILLARY. What about Henry?

CHARMAINE. Well, I was just talking with him when he suddenly burst into tears, complained about being hot, then dashed out into the garden.

(Enter **HENRY** *fanning himself.)*

HILLARY. There he is, let me talk to him. *(***CHARMAINE** *exits to B.R. 3, as* **HENRY** *comes D.) A*re you all right Henry? You don't look to well. You'd better sit down. *(***HENRY** *sits on the couch R. side as* **HILLARY** *sits on the couch L. side.)*

HENRY. I've been feeling very strange. Without warning my skin feels clammy and my body feels like it's on fire. I suddenly break out into an uncontrollable sweat, I feel like either breaking into tears, or yelling at the world, then, a moment later I'm fine. *(Almost wailing now.)* And why do I feel so fat? I know I'm not sick, I'm as healthy as a horse. It all started when I took one of those pills from Bud. He said they might have been a bad batch, and I think he could be right. Oh dear, here comes another one. *(Begins to tap his right foot, fan himself and pant.)*

HILLARY. What pills?

HENRY. You know, Bud's little blue pills.

HILLARY. You took one?

HENRY. Two. Don't ask, it's a long story.

HILLARY. You don't know the half of it.

HENRY. *(Stops fanning himself.)* What's that supposed to mean?

HILLARY. To make a long story short, we discovered that Bud was two-timing, correction, make that three-timing us women, so we devised a plot and swapped Bud's Viagra pills with the Venusia. Henry, what you took was your own *(Her voice trails off.)*...Venusia, I think the Venusia has given you female menopausal symptoms. What a riot, who would have thought it.

HENRY. You don't even care how I feel. What do you mean, what a riot, this isn't a riot, this is...this is awful. *(Breaks into tears)* You women are so insensitive.

HILLARY. *(Laughing.)* I think your more female than a female. You know, if you saw this on stage, no one would believe it.

HENRY. Do you realize just how hormonally challenged I am right now?

HILLARY. Come on Henry, it's not that bad. If it is true, at least you'll be back to normal when the pills wear off. We women can live with it for years. Incidentally, has Bud exhibited any of these same symptoms?

HENRY. Absolutely, all of them. *(Fanning himself.)* Oh, here I go again. *(Taps his R foot again.)*

HILLARY. Henry, do you realize what this means?

HENRY. It means I'm going to be hotter than hell again.

HILLARY. No Henry, you're going to be rich.

HENRY. What?

HILLARY. Every menopausal woman on the planet is going to want to buy Venusia to give to their unsympathetic husbands.

HENRY. Why? Why would anybody want to feel like this?

HILLARY. Exactly! Women will now have an opportunity to make men understand what we go through.

HENRY. It's all about women isn't it? You don't care that I'm feeling just terrible, you only think of yourselves. Oh…Oh….here I go again. *(Runs out the nook French doors fanning himself.)*

HILLARY. *(Crosses L. to BR 3, knocks,* CHARMAINE *enters)* I discovered what is wrong with Henry.

CHARMAINE. What?

HILLARY. *(Bursts into fits of giggles.)* He's menopausal.

CHARMAINE. What?

HILLARY. *(Crosses R. to BR 1 as* CHARMAINE *sits on the couch L.)* Hold on a minute, let me get Victoria.

CHARMAINE. Menopausal? Oh, I can't wait to hear this.

HILLARY. *(Knocks on the door of BR 1, enter* VICTORIA.*)* Hi, do you have a minute? I've got something to tell you.

VICTORIA. *(Follows* HILLARY *L. and sits on the couch R. as* HILLARY *sits in the chair.)* Sure, I needed a break anyways. So, what's up?

HILLARY. Henry is menopausal.

VICTORIA. What?

HILLARY. It appears that by accident Henry took some of his own Venusia pills, and it looks like the pills give men, female menopausal symptoms.

VICTORIA. What a riot.

CHARMAINE. Oh my stars and garters, why Bud was popping them faster than a pig eats pecans.

VICTORIA. Then Bud is menopausal too?

HILLARY. We can't be sure, but probably. Henry was having hot flashes, crying at the drop of a hat, cranky as all get out, feeling fat, and calling me insensitive.

VICTORIA. Well, that certainly sounds menopausal. What about Bud?

CHARMAINE. If right is right, that tomcat will get what's coming to him.

HILLARY. I understand that, but if Bud feels anything like

Henry, I can't help but feel sorry for him. I wouldn't wish menopausal symptoms on my worst enemy.

VICTORIA. Well, I don't feel that bad for them. Their symptoms are temporary, ours our permanent. Let them have a taste of what we go through. Maybe Bud will learn his lesson. *(Crosses R.)* I wish I could stay, but I need to get back to my writing. Thanks to you Charmaine, I'm almost done. *(Exits BR 1.)*

CHARMAINE. *(Crosses L.)* You know, if my granny was here today she'd say....why, I don't know what she'd say. This is stranger than grits without gravy. *(Exits BR 3.)*

*(Enter **BUD** from the D.R. French doors, very upset and deflated.)*

BUD. *(Muttering to himself.)* I just don't understand it, how can I be out of Viagra. I checked my pill supplies just yesterday, I think. I don't remember having that many chicks. Then again, my memory's going...oh, Ms. Hudson, hello. *(Starts to fan himself, then slumps down into the couch R.)*

HILLARY. Why Bud, you don't look so well. *(Enter **HENRY** from the nook French doors.)* What...no caviar, no roses, no....

HENRY. *(Crosses DSC and sits on the couch L.)* Hillary, stop pestering Bud, can't you see he's hormonally challenged right now?

HILLARY. *(Stands.)* Why Henry, didn't you take your cranky pill today? Don't you think you'd better tell Bud what's happening to him? *(Exits BR. 2.)*

BUD. Tell Bud what?

HENRY. I'm afraid the Viagra pills you thought you took, were actually Venusia, and they appear to give men female menopausal symptoms. *(Starts to cry.)*

BUD. What?

HENRY. How many of them did you take?

BUD. *(Starts to weep.)* I lost count after six.

HENRY. Oh dear.

BUD. Oh dear?

HENRY. Oh dear, I'm afraid the pills have caused you to go from Bud the Stud to…

BUD. Bud the Dud. *(Weeping loudly.)* How long will this last? Will it go away? I just want it to go away.

HENRY. I'm not sure, but it's an all natural vegetable product, so it should eventually wear off…I hope *(Starts to mop his brow.)* Oh no, ….here I go again. *(Taps his right foot.)*

BUD. This is terrible Henry….how could you do this to me, I'm supposed to be a sex symbol.

HENRY. I didn't do this to you, you did this to yourself.

BUD. Sure, blame me. You are so insensitive. *(Starts to fan himself.)* I'm going all clammy again.

HENRY. I am so insensitive? It's all about you isn't it. You don't care how I feel.

BUD. *(Starts to cry.)* Feel…feel? OK….But why do I feel so bloated?

HENRY. Bud, listen to us, we sound just like women. *(Both **BUD** and **HENRY** weep loudly.)*

BUD. Well, I'm not going to just sit here and …*(Tries to stand, when suddenly his back goes out, leaving him in a bent over position.)* OOOOHHHH!

HENRY. What is it Bud?

BUD. My back is out again. Can you help?

HENRY. Oh no! Here comes another one. *(He taps his right foot and starts to fan himself again.)*

BUD. You just don't care do you. *(Bursts into tears again.)* Here I am practically paralyzed, and all you can think about is your stupid hot flash. If you're not going to help can you at least get Ms. Hudson.

HENRY. *(Gets up and goes to BR 2)* OK Bud, I'll get Ms. Hudson for you, but I think you're being very selfish, asking me to help you when I'm in this state. *(Knocks on the door and bursts into tears.)*

*(**HILLARY** opens the door as **HENRY**, really howling now, points to **BUD**)*

HILLARY. Oh, oh, not again. My poor Budly. *(Moves quickly to* **BUD***)* Henry, his back is out. If you're not going to help why don't you go get Charmaine to help me get him on the couch.

*(***HILLARY** *tries to support* **BUD***, and in doing so, does not see what happens to* **HENRY***.* **HENRY** *moves to the door of B.R. 3 and knocks, the door opens immediately.* **CHARMAINE** *opens the door, flings her arms around* **HENRY***'s neck, kisses him passionately on the lips, drags him into the room and closes the door.)*

BUD. I hope you can fix it like last time Ms. Hudson.

HILLARY. Oh my poor Budly. You really have had a bad day. I'll see what I can do. *(Looks around.)* Where the heck did Henry go? Here, let me see if I can help you. *(She puts her head and shoulder underneath his R. armpit.)* O.K., here we go, on the count of three One, two, three. *(They both straighten up.)*

BUD.*(Begins to weep again.)* I really do appreciate your help.

HILLARY. Do you really mean that or is that the Venusia talking?

BUD. Yes,…. I mean no, …I mean…Oh I'm so confused.

HILLARY. Bud, I think you're getting in touch with your sensitive side.

BUD. I didn't even know I had a sensitive side.

(The door to B.R. 3 opens, **HENRY** *staggers out and leans on the doorframe. He is now somewhat disheveled, with his shirt pulled out and big red kisses all over his face.* **CHARMAINE** *reappears in the doorway, puts her arms around his waist, and pulls him backwards into the room, closing the door.)*

HILLARY. *(Takes* **BUD***'s hand and leads him over to the couch. She sits R. and he sits L.)* You know Bud, I think your sensitive side makes you really cute and adorable.

BUD. You do?

HILLARY. *(Leans forward and runs her fingers through his hair.)* You're really a very attractive man when you're not making up all those phony speeches.

BUD. I am?

HILLARY. Absolutely, any woman would be proud to be seen with you.

BUD. They would?

HILLARY. *(Gives him a kiss on the cheek.)* Of course they would.

*(The door to B.R. 3 opens, and **HENRY** appears in the doorway. His pants belt is undone, his zipper down, and his pants down on his hips. As he steps into the room, we see **CHARMAINE** dragging behind him on the floor, clutching his pants, trying to pull them off, while **HENRY** is trying to pull them up. **CHARMAINE** now stands, and with one yank on his pants, pulls him back into the room, closing the door.)*

BUD. You are a very lovely woman, and I'm a little ashamed of the way I behaved yesterday. I hope you'll forgive me. *(Takes **HILLARY***'s hand in his and kisses it.)*

HILLARY. Why Bud, that's so sweet. Of course I do. Would you like to have dinner with me tonight?

BUD. I think perhaps I'd like to have dinner with you every night.

HILLARY. Why Bud! *(Goes to kiss him on the cheek, **BUD** quickly turns, and kisses her on the lips.)*

BUD. Hillary my dear, I think I'm in love. I'm afraid though that all that seems to be working today are my lips.

HILLARY. Oh Bud, I don't think we need to worry about that, look what I've got? *(Takes the Viagra bottle out of her pocket and waves it in front of him. She gets up, backs away to the door of B.R. 2. **BUD** follows like a dog on a leash and they pause by the door, as **VICTORIA** appears in the doorway of BR 1 and watches.)*

BUD. Bud the Stud is back in business.

HILLARY. Bud?

BUD. Er...er.... what I meant was...er...Bud the Stud is only doing business with you my heavenly Hillary. *(Turns and winks at the audience as he kisses **HILLARY***'s hand and twirls her into the room, closing the door.)*

VICTORIA. "I am yours forever," he whispered, as she led him towards a night of unbridled passion.

(The door to B.R. 3 opens, **HENRY** *appears fastening his belt and zipper. He runs, looks over his shoulder, then exits through the nook French windows.* **CHARMAINE** *enters from B.R. 3.)*

CHARMAINE. Why that Henry, he's more slippery than a well-oiled penny on a wet bar of soap. I felt about as welcome as a skunk at a lawn party.

VICTORIA. Oh Charmaine, I can't thank you enough. I have been writing and writing. I finished my manuscript and can't wait to start the next book. Oh, are you all right? You don't look very happy?

CHARMAINE. Well honey, that's because I've struck out here. You know, my granny always said, when the door closes, find an open window.

VICTORIA. So what are you going to do?

CHARMAINE. I'm fixin' to head back home. There's a young lawman in town I've had my eye on for some weeks now. Hey, have you ever thought about writing a modern romance in the heart of Dixie?

VICTORIA. Oh, what a great idea, but I don't know anything about the South.

CHARMAINE. Well better now than never. Come stay with me for a little while, you know I'll give you lots to write about.

VICTORIA. You've got it. Consider my bags packed.

CHARMAINE. Honey, when you get to Dixie, you're going to learn that us southern ladies aren't always ladies.

VICTORIA. And the gentlemen?

CHARMAINE. Aren't always gentlemen.

VICTORIA. That's it! You've just given me the title for my next book, "Sex Please We're Southern". *(Exits to B.R. 1.)*

CHARMAINE. Well, strip my gears and call me shiftless, I'm gonna be a leadin' lady in a romance novel. *(Exits to B.R. 3)*

(Re-enter **HENRY**, *now cleaned up, from the nook French doors. He carefully looks around, then pours himself a glass of wine. He is about to take a sip when* **MRS. STANCLIFFE** *enters from the office, now totally transformed. She is dressed in an elegant evening gown and high heels, her hair soft around her face, and wearing make-up and jewelry, and carrying a single red rose. She comes D.R. and closes the French doors, as* **HENRY** *stands watching her with his mouth wide open.* **MRS. STANCLIFFE** *turns U.S. and sees* **HENRY**.*)*

HENRY. *(Comes D.)* Is that you Buttercup? You look so different.

MRS. STANCLIFFE. I am different Henry. Do you like the new me?

HENRY. *(Comes D. and takes her hands in his.)* You are the most beautiful woman in the world. *(Drops down on one knee.)* Would you do me the honor…

MRS. STANCLIFFE. No Henry, please get up. *(*HENRY *stands as* **MRS. STANCLIFFE** *goes down on one knee.)* Oh my handsome Henry, please accept this rose as a token of my love for you. Will you marry me?

HENRY. *(Helps her up.)* Oh my beautiful Buttercup. *(They embrace and kiss.)*

CURTAIN

FURNITURE AND PROPERTY LIST

ON STAGE

Reception counter. ON IT: Computer notebook. Call bell. Telephone.
An empty vase with water. BEHIND IT: Reservation forms. Pen. Keys.
Large potted plant.
A round table.
Three chairs.
A buffet. ON IT: Pitcher of iced-tea. Glasses.
A sofa.
Low back easy chair.
End table.
Paintings.
Drapes.
A vase of fresh flowers.

ACT I OFFSTAGE

A basket of fresh cut flowers. Scissors. (MRS. STANCLIFFE)
Bouquet of carnations. (HENRY)
Pill bottle with pills. (HENRY)
Computer bag. IN IT: Printed pages. Small suitcase. (VICTORIA)
Small suitcase. Purse. (HILLARY)
Champagne. Roses. (BUD)
Bouquet pansies. (HENRY)
Small suitcase. Purse. (CHARMAINE)
Red Wine. Roses. (BUD)
Tray of sandwiches. Bottle of wine. Wine glasses. (MRS. STANCLIFFE)
Roses with a card. Champagne. Caviar. (BUD)

ACT II OFFSTAGE

Basket of flowers. Scissors. (MRS. STANCLIFFE)
Walker. (BUD)
Huge bouquet of assorted flowers. (HENRY)
Pill bottle with pills. (HILLARY)
Large Teddy Bear (HENRY)
Pad. Pencil. (VICTORIA)
Red rose. (MRS. STANCLIFFE)

PERSONAL

Pen. (HENRY)
Pill bottle with pills. (BUD)
Handkerchief. (HENRY)
Note paper. (HENRY)
Pencil. (HENRY)
Handkerchief. (BUD)

COSTUMES

BUD
Short sleeve plaid shirt.
Khaki pants.
Sweater vest.
Golf cap.
Dress shoes and socks.
Boxer shorts with red hearts.
Sport shirt with collar.
Suspenders.

HENRY
2 different colored polo shirts.
Khaki pants.
Dress shoes and socks.

HILLARY
Designer summer suit with skirt.
Blouse.
Accessories and shoes to match.
Sensuous lounge wear.
Casual summer skirt and top
Sandals.

MRS. STANCLIFFE
Long plain dress.
Ankle boots.
Garden gloves.
A watch.
Long dress with color.
Elegant evening gown.
High heels.
Accessories to match.

VICTORIA
Modest summer dress.
Accessories and shoes to match.
Peignoir set.
Blouse.
Cotton pants.
Flat shoes.

CHARMAINE
2 elegant, low cut summer
dresses.
High heeled sandals.
Accessories to match.
Short nightie.

SEX PLEASE WE'RE SIXTY

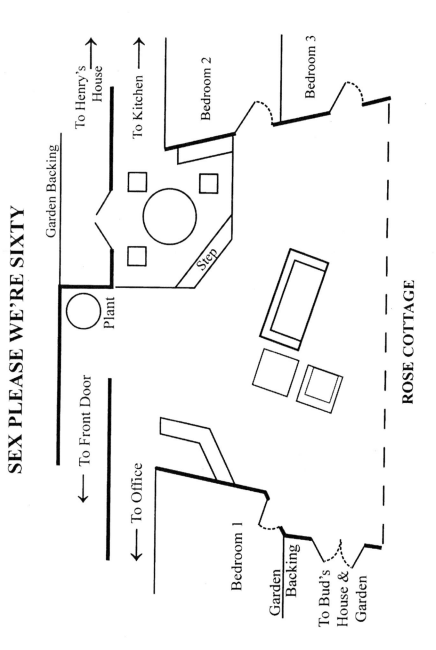

Garden Backing

To Henry's House

To Kitchen

Bedroom 2

Bedroom 3

Plant

Step

To Front Door

To Office

Bedroom 1

Garden Backing

To Bud's House & Garden

ROSE COTTAGE

Also by
Michael Parker...

The Amorous Ambassador

Hotbed Hotel

The Lone Star Love Potion

The Sensuous Senator

There's a Burglar in My Bed

Who's in Bed with the Butler?

Whose Wives Are They Anyway?

Never Kiss a Naughty Nanny

And

Sin, Sex & The C.I.A.

By Michael Parker and Susan Parker

LaVergne, TN USA
12 February 2010
172817LV00001B/20/P